Meg Elison

Winner of the
Philip K. Dick Award
Twice nominated for the
Tiptree Award

on *The Book of the Unnamed Midwife*

"A strikingly powerful story . . . An apocalyptic page-turner that picks up where *The Handmaid's Tale* left off."
—Jackie Hatton, Tor.com

"An honest novel, both in the way it depicts a postapocalyptic world and how it recognizes that human sexuality and the need to fuck and feel pleasure will stay with us even as the human race falls into darkness."
—Ian Mond, *Locus* magazine

"One of the most utterly absorbing books I've read in a long time . . . Grim but lots of pockets of warmth. Really interesting protagonist, an unnamed midwife, who begins to create a written history that will survive her for generations. Loved this novel."
—Roxane Gay, author of *Bad Feminist*

on *The Book of Flora*

"An urgent, ferociously readable warning about the power of belief to maim—or heal. Readers will find this a powerful conclusion to a fascinating series."
—*Publishers Weekly*

Big Girl

plus

PM PRESS OUTSPOKEN AUTHORS SERIES

1. *The Left Left Behind*
   Terry Bisson

2. *The Lucky Strike*
   Kim Stanley Robinson

3. *The Underbelly*
   Gary Phillips

4. *Mammoths of the Great Plains*
   Eleanor Arnason

5. *Modem Times 2.0*
   Michael Moorcock

6. *The Wild Girls*
   Ursula K. Le Guin

7. *Surfing the Gnarl*
   Rudy Rucker

8. *The Great Big Beautiful Tomorrow*
   Cory Doctorow

9. *Report from Planet Midnight*
   Nalo Hopkinson

10. *The Human Front*
    Ken MacLeod

11. *New Taboos*
    John Shirley

12. *The Science of Herself*
    Karen Joy Fowler

13. *Raising Hell*
    Norman Spinrad

14. *Patty Hearst & The Twinkie Murders: A Tale of Two Trials*
    Paul Krassner

15. *My Life, My Body*
    Marge Piercy

PM PRESS OUTSPOKEN AUTHORS SERIES

16. *Gypsy*
Carter Scholz

17. *Miracles Ain't What They Used to Be*
Joe R. Lansdale

18. *Fire.*
Elizabeth Hand

19. *Totalitopia*
John Crowley

20. *The Atheist in the Attic*
Samuel R. Delany

21. *Thoreau's Microscope*
Michael Blumlein

22. *The Beatrix Gates*
Rachel Pollack

23. *A City Made of Words*
Paul Park

24. *Talk like a Man*
Nisi Shawl

25. *Big Girl*
Meg Elison

26. *The Planetbreaker's Son*
Nick Mamatas

Big Girl

plus

The Pill

plus

Such People in It

and much more

Meg Elison

PM PRESS | 2020

"El Hugé" was originally published in *Catapult*, 2017 (catapult.co).

"Gone with *Gone with the Wind*" was originally published as "How I Bought into *Gone with the Wind*'s Mythology of Whiteness" in *Electric Literature*, 2018 (electricliterature.com).

"Guts" was originally published as "My Friends Would Rather Have Their Guts Cut Open Than Be Like Me" in *The Establishment*, 2019 (theestablishment.co).

"Big Girl" was originally published in *Fantasy & Science Fiction*, November–December 2017.

"The Pill" and "Such People in It" are original to this volume.

Big Girl
Meg Elison © 2020
This edition © PM Press

ISBN (paperback): 978-1-62963-783-9
ISBN (ebook): 978-1-62963-810-2
LCCN: 2019946142

Series editor: Terry Bisson
Cover design by John Yates/www.stealworks.com
Author photograph by Debbie Reynolds, Libre Images
Insides by Jonathan Rowland

10 9 8 7 6 5 4 3 2 1

Printed in the USA

CONTENTS

El Hugé   1

Big Girl   5

The Pill   23

Gone with *Gone with the Wind*   63

Such People in It   73

"Sprawling into the Unknown"   93
Meg Elison interviewed by Terry Bisson

Guts   105

Bibliography   113

About the Author   115

El Hugé

WHEN I WAS FIFTEEN, I slew a giant that had done me no harm. I had to do it. There was no other way. I lived in the kind of town that nobody believes exists anymore. An hour from any freeway, we were surrounded by oranges on one side and cows on the other, with tumbleweed traversing the valley when the wind kicked up. This wasn't Oklahoma, it was southern California.

In a yearly culmination of a fall harvest festival—because Halloween is pagan and somehow a harvest is not—farmers from all over the valley brought in the biggest pumpkins they had grown. There were no prohibitions on performance-enhancing drugs in this squash Olympics; people tried everything from Miracle-Gro to burying their gently radioactive Fiestaware in the dirt. The pumpkins grew monstrous, sloping and misshapen, formless under their own mass. Their coloring was like cancerous flesh. They had no beauty, only bigness.

The biggest one that year was El Hugé (*hugh-gay*); over twelve hundred pounds of pale, ghoulish, inedible pumpkin. The farmer took a blue ribbon and the paper got his picture. The gourd sat out in the Indian summer heat on public display.

In the purpling night, long after school had ended, I sat forgotten at the edge of a parking lot. I was debating whether to give up and try sleeping at a friend's house, or to keep waiting for someone who was likely never coming. My indecision was broken by a guy named Cole, dangerous and sexy at seventeen, with a scar like someone had dripped hot candle wax out of his eye socket and onto his cheek. He drove a beat-up black pickup truck with red duct tape playing understudy to taillights. I didn't think twice when he told me to get in.

I was the kind of girl who would have slept with him for a smaller kindness, but that wasn't what he was after. We picked up two of his friends, black-leather types, who crawled into the jump-out seats wedged behind us in the cab of the truck. One friend carried a swollen backpack that Cole referred to as "the supplies."

"Supplies for what?" I asked, hoping that I was at least going to be subjected to peer pressure over drugs and alcohol. My peers had something else in mind.

"For El Hugé."

The pumpkin had not been named by the farmer or the newspaper. It was one of those things that just arrived one day, like an urban legend that everyone knows but no one can trace. Bad Spanish is a badge of honor among poor whites living in what was once Mexico, and so El Hugé was his name.

I didn't protest. I didn't suggest that this might be a bad idea. When the boys lined up long pieces of lumber to build a ramp and began to push the pumpkin into the bed of the truck, I jumped out and put my back into it.

Somehow, we loaded the thing. The truck groaned and the shocks were compressed. One of the tires scraped in its wheel well as we crept out of the larceny lot. But we got away.

In a dry riverbed, miles out of town, we shoved our vegetal hostage back out onto the ground. It settled malevolently on its flat side.

I don't know how we came to this conclusion because not a word was said, but we hated El Hugé. That pumpkin's existence was somehow inexcusably offensive to us. Cole outlined a crude jack-o'-lantern face on its ghost-orange skin, and one of the other boys stabbed the sappy adipose flesh with a long knife he had stolen from his mother's kitchen.

We couldn't cut a face. It took our combined strength to sink or remove the knife, and we were soon exhausted.

Cole looked over our handiwork and said that surely if we punched the face out with a dotted line like a coupon, we could blow the cutouts from within. We who had been instructed in almost no science reasoned the idea would probably work and set about stabbing a pattern into the widest side of El Hugé.

Cole made an incision near the stem with a shovel, standing on the mountainous pumpkin and flailing a little for his balance. When he had dug a hole, he motioned for the backpack.

Night had fallen for real and the butane perfume and flare of his Zippo were a shock in the cool air. He lit a handful of M-80s and thrust them down into El Hugé's brainpan. He leapt off the top, rolling on the gravel. We ran and took shelter behind the pickup truck. We waited.

There is something in the soul of mediocrity that seeks to stomp down anyone or anything that stands out. There is something in us small-town kids that makes us lobsters, pulling each other back into a bucket so that no one gets out. We weren't going to be outdone by a pumpkin. We weren't going to outdo it, either. What could we do but destroy its beauty in the crudest, most fumbling form we could muster? We were children, and we were unremarkable and unloved. That beloved pumpkin had to die.

The explosion was muffled, yet sizeable. To our surprise, a neatly punched face did not pop prettily free to reveal a jack-o'-lantern as tall as our shoulders. Instead, El Hugé collapsed, a giant hole at his top and another at his bottom. Hot seeds and guts rolled out along the underside, as if we had disemboweled an ungulate. The top was a mystery to us until flaming pumpkin chunks began to rain down, slapping into the black truck and coating us with hot, stinking gourd innards.

We were filthy and terrified, but we had won. No one ever found out what became of El Hugé; the papers casually remarked upon its theft, blaming the perennial scourge of teenagers. Years later, I went back to that riverbed and found a wide patch of stubborn, ugly pumpkins growing on surly vines.

Big Girl

THE GIRL WOKE UP with a sore neck and three seagulls perched on her eyelashes.

As her eyes fluttered open, the startled gulls flapped away. They squawked in alarm, but continued on in the gray predawn light.

She shook her head a little, still not fully awake. She blinked a few times, and the men on the fishing boat saw a chunk of yellow sleep-crust the size of a bike tire fall from her eye and splash in the water beside them. As she stepped into the water, the boat rocked as if it were passing through the wake of a much larger ship. She blundered forward, slipping and falling to her knees. The impact registered as a 3.1 on a nearby seismograph, and the wave pushed the boat out to the end of its anchor chain.

Her dark hair hung over her face, but when she began to wail her disorientation, it blew out in front of her mouth like black banners caught in the wind. The fishermen pulled their anchor in a panic. The girl stood up to her full height, towering over the Richmond Bridge. Apparently realizing that she was naked, she covered herself with her arms.

She was still standing there with her arms crossed tight over her breasts when the first helicopters arrived.

SFGate.com

Reports are coming in that a huge inflatable sex doll has been spotted floating near the Richmond Bridge. Tweet sightings or pics to @SFGate.

San Francisco Chronicle

Early reports of an inflatable woman or large art installation near the Richmond Bridge this morning have been confirmed via independent footage acquired by the *Chronicle* today. The drone video shows that the object is animated, some speculate by radio control. The object resembles a human female and is approximately 350 feet tall. The figure is nude and has no obvious brand logos or other marks identifying its provenance.

Video and still photos indicate that the object is anchored or perhaps confined to the area immediately surrounding Red Rock Island. There are reports from boats in the vicinity that the figure is broadcasting sound, though it is unknown whether it is issuing music or recorded statements.

So far, no artist or corporation has claimed ownership of or responsibility for the appearance of the phenomenon. This may be due to the controversial nudity of the figure, which appears to be very lifelike and anatomically correct.

More on this story as it develops.

@kindnesskillzzz: I saw the #baybe this morning, there's no way it's inflatable, too lifelike.

@3librasalad: hey @USCG is approaching #baybe right now. *Image: a U.S. Coast Guard vessel pulls in front of a light-brown calf, kneecap visible above ship's antennas.*

@USCG: All vessels and individuals steer clear of #baybe phenomenon until further notice. We are assessing the safety of the situation.

@SFExaminer: The #baybe is a real girl! Sources have identified Bianca Martinez of East Oakland, age 15. sfexnews/lgt5hjY

It took a couple of hours to corroborate the *Examiner*'s scoop. No one believed their claim that the girl was human and assumed the headline was a hoax or a hack. By the time the truth hit the news, thousands of pictures had been taken of the girl huddled beside a Coast Guard boat, goosebumps as large as Canada geese all over her blue-brown skin.

East Bay Express
In the first few days after the Baybe (Bianca Martinez, a fifteen-year-old Oakland girl) appeared in the water, misinformation ruled.

Between reports that she was an inflatable art project, a publicity stunt, or a pre-Burning Man exhibition of an animatronic sculpture, the truth remained elusive.

Yet, as Joel Rabinowitz at the *SF Examiner* first reported and the Coast Guard later confirmed, Ms. Martinez is a human female. More than that, she's a minor. Once positive identification was made and her DNA was matched with that of her parents, publishing or selling photos of the nude colossus became illegal.

Photos have been surrendered to and seized by local police and the FBI, but the Internet is keeping the images alive in an echo of the Fappening back in 2014. Far from being leaked or hacked, however, most of these photos were taken by legitimate journalists and printed in nationally circulated newspapers, on TV news, and on Twitter. Getting this unexpected tidal wave of child pornography under control is now as difficult as housing or feeding the Baybe herself.

Alameda County Child Welfare has stepped in, attempting to help Martinez's parents provide for their child's gigantic needs. The struggle to clothe her attracted donations of sailcloth and large nautical tarps, but the girl still appears to be only half-clothed and constantly shivering. Food banks claimed record donations as people banded together to feed Martinez, but county officials struggled to find her somewhere to eat where people cannot crowd around to watch. The solution thus far has involved Martinez wading into the Bay to eat out of her hands in relative privacy.

Experts have estimated Martinez's height at somewhere around 350 feet and her weight at almost 100 tons. Her passage across the Bay has disrupted ferry and fishing boat traffic, and the Coast Guard has issued a ban on all sailboats and small craft for the time being.

Martinez was seen only two nights ago batting dozens of drones out of the air around her, sweeping them into the sea to avoid their lights and cameras. In the carefully cropped picture that ran on the front page, pixelated starfish dotted the edge of her pubic hair like deliberate decoration. The *East Bay Express* attempted to find out where the Baybe sleeps, but our search came up empty.

BuzzFeed

Is San Francisco's giant mystery girl human?

Human rights organizations around the world are struggling with this question now as government officials on all sides hesitate to offer the girl, Bianca Martinez, any kind of aid.

"She's just so damned big," Oakland mayor Laney Schiff remarked. "It's difficult to think of her as a citizen of Oakland when Oakland can't begin to meet her needs. And as she's taken up temporary indigent residence on various beaches and islands, I'm not sure it's strictly Oakland's issue."

A representative from the Department of Human Services said the organization was unclear on their responsibilities in this case. "She is fifteen, and she was a completely normal-sized girl a week ago. But today, tomorrow, who knows? We're waiting on a decision as to how we should deal with this."

Samuel Sapporo, one of Martinez's former teachers at Oakland High, offered another point of view, saying, "Imagine if this was your kid. She's terrified and exposed and there's nowhere safe for her to go. She's homeless and naked and practically starving, and we're going to argue whether she's a person anymore?"

Oakland Police are concerned about Martinez's superhuman strength and abilities. One officer, who asked not to be named, said, "What if she decides to walk home one day? She might flatten Chinatown, maybe knock out the MacArthur Maze while she's at it. She could destroy some BART tracks, and we couldn't do anything to stop her. That's not a person; that's a threat."

Martinez's parents are reported to have limited English proficiency and have thus far refused to speak with the press. The

Coast Guard arranged for them to visit their daughter on a boat last Monday, but the boat reportedly never left the dock. A source close to the family said the parents are struggling to cope. Martinez's father is a plumber and her mother is a homemaker. The family attends Our Lady of Lourdes Catholic Church, but have not been spotted there in recent weeks.

Representatives of the Oakland diocese declined to comment on Bianca Martinez's humanity.

[redacted].net (excerpt)

Why am I being harassed by the FBI and other law enforcement for posting pictures of this hot-ass teen giant? She's a big girl. She looks grown-up to me. For fuck's sake, she could crush my skull with her thumb—can she really be a victim? Talk about unrape-able. Kiss me goodbye and flick me to Oregon if I climbed up that mountain of round ass.

[redacted].com (excerpt)

Nobody inched along the giant's neck, taking measured little steps. Her breathing was like a hot wind that caressed him all over, whistling around his erection like a breeze through the trees.

"Who's there?" she rumbled in her huge, deep voice.

"Nobody," Nobody said, trembling.

"Oh, I don't think so. You can't fool Mommy like that." The giant pinched Nobody around the thigh and lifted him high in the air. He screamed in ecstasy and terror. She dropped him into her massive maw and swallowed him whole.

He was engulfed in the warm, wet folds of her enormous throat. Muscles worked all around him, forcing him downward, squeezing him tight. He slipped into the total darkness of the giant's stomach, the acidic heat suffusing him with deadly desire.

Nobody felt along the stomach lining until he found a comfortable, groovy place to grind his aching member against her pulsing insides.

The giant gurgled happily in her sleep.

@WTFFFacts: Bianca Martinez, the giantess of the SF Bay, has a heart as big and as heavy as a Volkswagen Beetle.

@BarelyLegal99: Countdown to Bianca Martinez's 18th birthday: bit.ly/ 98yTpA3

New York Times

I first met Bianca Martinez sitting on the beach in Marin County. She had been shot several times by park rangers after an altercation involving the now-deceased photographer Mark Hanhofer. Ms. Martinez, in her attempt to stop him from photographing her genitals close-up as she slept, pulled Hanhofer's left arm off his body. He died immediately from blood loss.

Bianca sat cross-legged on the pebbled beach, squeezing bullets out of the skin of her forearm like a patch of blackheads. She had to whisper to me; anything louder was overwhelming. There was no hope of privacy.

I asked her if she was under arrest.

She shrugged her massive shoulders, a hypnotic, rippling, rising and falling wall of flesh. "They say I am, but they can't cuff me or put me in jail. So I guess I'm 'in trouble.'" At this, she made air quotes with two fingers, each the size of a full-grown dolphin. She glanced over at the park rangers, her brown eye as big as the driver's side window. "I guess they could chain me to something. Maybe."

In the days that followed, she was approached by several different branches of law enforcement, as well as DHS. The helplessness they shared was palpable as they failed to come to a decision on how to govern the giant girl's behavior. In the end, they decided that she had killed the photographer in self-defense and gave up, driving their squad cars and sport-utility vehicles off the beach. The two of us were left with the gulls and the constant sound of drones trying to come near enough to film her while staying out of reach.

I asked her what she missed. With her massive face laid on the warm rocks beside me, she whispered things that any teenage girl might name.

"My friends," she said as an elephantine tear slid down her face to pool on the rocks. "My school. My clothes. I miss wearing clothes so much. I'm cold all the time. Nothing anybody has offered is even close to big enough. I just hold it against me. I dream every night that I'm back in my bed, but then I wake up and it's raining."

Yesterday, Karl the Fog, the popular personification of the ever-present San Francisco fog, tweeted at Bianca that he would like to marry her. The last time I saw her, she stood up on that beach and made for the Marin Headlands, a wooded area sparsely populated by some of the richest people in the state. Local papers report that homeowners there fear her presence and the possible damage she might do. As she reared up to her full, terrible height, the fog wrapped itself around her like the soft gray fur of an arctic fox.

Karl might be the only match for this monster of a girl.

@buttstuffedpizza: I went to school with Bianca since we were eight. I feel so bad for her.

@candleinthewind: this has gone on long enough someone needs to help her #baybe

@giantsfan87: We finally have a real SF Giant! Too bad she's got cramps and can't play.

@BBCBreaking: Bianca Martinez, the giant of San Francisco Bay, found unresponsive on the beach. bbc.in/uG5hk6

@oaktownratz: BEACHED WHALE! *[Image redacted]*

San Francisco Chronicle

Bianca Martinez, the Bay Area's mysterious giant girl, was found unresponsive, lying on the beach near Point Richmond yesterday evening. Footage from the KPIX newscopter shows that her abdomen is slightly distended and she is bleeding from her vaginal area. Attempts to rouse her by sound or pressure applied by car have failed. Her parents were present, along with their priest, who reportedly gave the girl last rites sometime after sundown.

EMTs on the scene detected Martinez's pulse and confirmed that she was still alive but could not determine the cause of her unconsciousness. Attempts to cover Martinez's body or move it back from the encroaching surf have failed.

Snapchat Story: She's So Heavy (SF)

An EMT in whites takes Martinez's pulse by leaning against her neck, forearms pressed to the skin, head turned away from the massive body as he tries to count. The vibrations of her pulse bob his head slightly, slowly.

A crowd of girls in UC Berkeley gear pose a few feet from the body, smiling until one of them realizes her shoe is sinking into the bloody sand.

Martinez slowly lifts one hand, its shadow passing over the morning beach walkers and their dogs. All heads turn. A woman screams and her small dog barks self-importantly, punctuating the sound.

Martinez's hand drops into the surf and the giant rises. She drags her knees through the wet sand, digging trenches large enough to drive a Jeep into. Her right hand leaves a perfect print as she pushes up off the beach.

Caked sand falls from her breasts and belly as she reaches her full height. Chunks come raining down, smashing apart on the ground when they hit. Cameras trained on her face pick up only a black shape against the early-morning light.

The giant walks into the sea, washing away blood and sand, saying nothing.

sfgiantwatch.com

It's been 413 days since we last had a sighting of Bianca the Giant.

Rumors that she has fled to the Farallón Islands remain unsubstantiated. The islands are out of drone range and no ship has spotted her or brought back pictures. Aircraft have not been able to locate her.

Is it possible she's dead? Did she just walk into the sea? We need answers.

The giant belongs to all of us. She's a symbol of the fantastic, the awesome, the unknowable reach of human potential.

Every time a lighthouse on the Bay makes its circle, I hope she knows it's searching for her.

California State Department of Justice: Featured Missing Children

Name: Bianca Rosalba Martinez
Report type: Runaway juvenile
Sex: Female
Race: Hispanic
Hair: Brown
Eyes: Brown
Height: 370 ft.
Weight: 200,000 lb.
Date of birth: 8/16/2002
Clothing: None
Last seen: 8/28/2017
Dental X-rays available: No

Bianca Martinez was last seen on the beach near the Sutro Baths.

Bianca didn't know the name of the island she was on, only that she had it to herself. There were caves and rock formations on one side, flat beach on the other. She caught dolphins that wriggled helplessly between her fingers and cried while she dashed their heads against the rocks to kill them. She didn't know how to light a fire. In time, she learned to deal with their raw flesh in her mouth.

She cracked whole coconuts between her teeth and cherished the warm drips of milk and sweet flesh. She tried not to eat them all but could not help herself. She caught tangles of kelp and ate that, too, hoping it was like a vegetable. It was salty and she hated it. She grew thin.

She watched the sun come up alone and go down occasionally in the company of the moon. She slept during the day, her broad brown back soaking up the sun. She walked the island at night, building sand castles two stories tall.

She tried to befriend seabirds, offering them shreds of fish and letting them walk on her hands. They shat on her and kept to themselves.

She thought she would die of loneliness, but every time she lay down she would wake as soon as she got cold.

She jumped at the sound of airplanes.

Almost two years had passed on the islands before she realized something was wrong. The seagulls in her palm were getting larger. Dolphins were too big to eat; she left parts strewn on the sand and watched crabs and flies swarm over them.

She tried to measure herself against the rocks, gauging whether she could see over the top from one day to the next.

The change had happened overnight the first time. This time, it crept into her body like a thief. She doubted it was real; she had wished for it too often. But the day came when she was shorter than the rock she could see over only a month before.

It took days for her to gather the courage to take to the water again. She had swum out to this place when she was too big for anything to stop her, too huge to care about any obstacle.

She knew there were things in the sea bigger than herself. She acclimated herself to daylight and chose a morning with a clear sky.

It took half the day to swim back. The pull of the tide yanked her farther and farther south. She came ashore in Monterey Bay, exhausted and with seawater in her lungs.

Santa Cruz Record

Santa Cruz police positively identified Bianca Martinez yesterday after her spectacular reemergence from hiding. The girl formerly known as the Baybe has shrunk substantially, coming in at only 100 feet tall. Local government officials scrambled to help her, noting that she has lost a considerable amount of weight and her massive ribs and hip bones are very prominent in her frame.

The Walnut Avenue Family and Women's Shelter has offered to assist Ms. Martinez, securing transitional housing and food donations for her. At her reduced size, they were also able to offer her something resembling clothing and she is said to be resting comfortably in a large structure somewhere in Santa Cruz County.

Experts are baffled as to why the Baybe has suddenly lost so much of her famous mass, and police report that the girl herself could offer no explanation. More on this story as it develops.

Hangar Inventory
2 pallets dry goods, donated by Grocery Outlet, contents unknown
16 king-size sheet sets, salvaged from Hotel Durant fire sale
2,000 gallons water, donated by Home Depot
2 pitchforks, donated by Home Depot
35 books, large print, donated by Santa Cruz Public Library
1 case Hershey bars, donated by Hershey
1 iPad, donated by Apple

Instagram account belonging to @streetprophetesss, 2,875 likes
Image: Bianca Martinez kneels between two A-frame ladders, seen from the back. Two women wielding pitchforks labor at detangling her hair, which hangs to her waist.
Caption: Every girl deserves to feel pretty! #justgirlythings #baybe #browneyedgirl

KPIX-TV News
Footage of Bianca Martinez emerging from her hangar rolls as a reporter speaks.

"It's coming-out day here in San Francisco as Bianca Martinez, the so-called Baybe, has agreed for the first time to speak on camera. We're all here, watching with bated breath as she approaches. As you can see, Martinez is much smaller than she used to be and is now able to wear clothes. It looks like she's about to reach the microphones—let's listen to what she has to say."

The reporter turns her back as the camera switches to a view of Bianca, microphones tiny in front of her chin. She opens her mouth, but no sound is heard. After a few moments of this, her face grows confused. The reporter turns to the camera again.

"It looks like we have a slight technical difficulty here. Let's take a moment and review the history of the Baybe phenomenon while the crew works it out."

Footage rolls from Bianca's debut, blurs and black bars obscuring her nudity. The prepared clips end but the audio has not improved. Bianca turns her back and crouches to reenter the hangar. No further word is issued.

@dev4dev4: Man, now #baybe wears clothes? Who authorized this?

@veryslimitude: Did anybody else notice that Bianca isn't as hot as she used to be?

@redlizardy: I wonder if the #baybe is going to be normal sized again. Can she just go back home? Is that allowed?

Bianca noticed her sheets were bigger and bigger on her every day. She woke up disoriented, unable to balance. Her hair was far too long, tickling the backs of her thighs.

When she was only twenty feet tall, she walked home. Cameras and drones followed, but not as many as before. She hardly noticed.

SF Examiner

Baybe has babe!

Bianca Martinez, the girl formerly known as the Baybe, gave birth to her first child today at Kaiser Permanente Medical Center in Oakland. At 15 feet 3 inches, Martinez is the tallest woman ever to have given birth. Her daughter, Inez, was born weighing eight pounds exactly and is only 18 inches long.

The child's father, Ricky Arden, a 32-year-old man from Oakland, laughed and joked with reporters this morning when asked about the birth.

"She just slid out!" Arden exclaimed, offering a gesture to illustrate. "She was so little, and Bianca is so big! Must be the easiest baby ever born."

Ms. Martinez was unavailable for comment. However, a source from the hospital informed us that Martinez left the hospital two feet shorter than she was at intake.

When Ricky left, Bianca was just over six and a half feet tall. Inez was four years old, perfectly normal and well adjusted in every way. She had not been close to her father and did not miss him for long.

It was Inez who pointed out to Bianca how short she was getting. Bianca's parents never liked to remark on her size. They had accepted her back home the day she was able to fit into their house again and never talked about the intervening years. But there was no denying it when Bianca's ten-year-old daughter grew taller than she was.

The mark on the wall said 4'11", but Bianca disliked numbers.

The college fund had come through anonymous donors years before, intended for Bianca herself. She had never gotten around to using it, but the people at the bank said yes, she could use it for her daughter, too. They had to put a box of computer paper on the floor to help her climb into the upholstered chair to sign her name.

The counselor at CSU Hayward was very sensitive to people with disabilities and went out of her way to make Ms. Martinez feel welcome. She had never registered a student whose parent was a little person, and the double minority status made her giddy as she entered Inez's information into the computer.

When Bianca got back to her car after dropping Inez off in her first dorm room, she found that her pedal extender was too short to reach the gas. She had to adjust the length to drive herself home, sitting up on her booster seat and peering over the dash.

Inez was the last person to see her mother. She came home one day in her sophomore year with a bursting laundry bag to find Bianca pacing back and forth across the wide pages of her scrapbook. It lay open to the images she had printed off the Internet: her own towering silhouette beside the Bay Bridge. Her feet made no impression as she walked across the heavy paper and back, no taller than a dragonfly.

Inez reached out her hand, unsure if she could touch her mother without hurting her.

"I'm in here somewhere," Bianca said.

The next day, try as she might, Inez could not find her mother at all.

The Pill

MY MOTHER TOOK THE Pill before anybody even knew about it. She was always signing up for those studies at the university, saying she was doing it because she was bored. I think she did it because they would ask her questions about herself and listen carefully when she answered. Nobody else did that.

She had done it for lots of trials; sleep studies and allergy meds. She tried signing up when they tested the first 3D-printed IUDs, but they told her she was too old. I remember her raging about that for days, and later when everybody in that study got fibroids she was really smug about it. She never suggested I do it instead; she knew I wasn't fucking anybody. How embarrassing that my own mother didn't even believe I was cute enough to get a date at sixteen. I tried not to care. And I'm glad now I didn't get fibroids. I never wanted to be a lab rat anyway. Especially when the most popular studies (and the ones Mom really went all-out for) were the diet ones.

She did them all: the digital calorie monitors that she wore on her wrists and ankles for six straight weeks. (I rolled my eyes at that one, but at least she didn't talk about it constantly.) The strings like clear licorice made of some kind of super-cellulose that were supposed to accumulate in her stomach lining and give her a no-surgery stomach stapling but just made her (and everyone else who didn't eat a placebo) fantastically constipated. (Unstoppable complaining about this one; I couldn't bring anyone home for weeks for fear that she'd abruptly start telling my friends about her struggle to shit.) Pill after pill after pill that gave her heart palpitations, made her hair fall out, or (on one memorable occasion) induced psychotic delusions. If it was a way out of being fat, she'd try it. She'd try anything.

In between the drug trials, she did all the usual diets. Eat like a caveman. Eat like a rabbit. Seven small meals. Fasting one day a week. Apple cider vinegar bottles with dust on their upper domes sat tucked into the back corners of our every kitchen cabinet, behind the bulwark of Fig Newmans and Ritz crackers.

She'd try putting the whole family on a diet, talk us into taking "family walks" in the evening. She'd throw out all the junk food and make us promise to love ourselves more. Loving yourself means crying over the scale every morning and then sniffling into half a grapefruit, right? Nothing stuck and nothing made any real difference. We all resisted her, eating in secret in our rooms or out of the house. I found Dad's bag of fish taco wrappers jammed under the driver's seat of the car while looking for my headphones. Mom caught me putting it in the garbage and yelled at me for like an hour. I never told her it was his. She was always hardest on me about my weight, as if I was the only one who had this problem. We were a fat family. Mom was just as fat as me; we looked like we were built to the same specs. Dad was fat, and my brother was the fattest of us all.

I'm still fat. Everyone else is in the past tense.

And why? Because of this fucking Pill.

That trial started the same way they always do: flyers all over campus where Mom worked, promising cash for the right demographic for an exciting new weight-loss solution. Mom jumped on it like she always did, taking a pic of the poster so she could email from the comfort of her broken-down armchair with the TV tray rolled up close and her laptop permanently installed there. I remember I asked her once why she even had a laptop if she never took it anywhere. She never even unplugged it! It might as well have been an old-school tower and monitor rig. Why go portable if you're never going to leave the port?

She shrugged. "Why call it a laptop when I don't have a lap?"

She had me there. I could never sit my computer in my "lap" either. That real estate was taken up by my belly when I sat, and it was terribly uncomfortable to have a screen down that low, anyway. I've seen people do it on the train, and they look all hunched and bent. But mom wanted the hunching and the bending. She wanted a flat, empty lap and a hot computer balanced on her knees. She wanted inches of clearance between her hips and an airline seat and to buy the clothes she saw on the mannequin in the window. She wanted what everybody wants. Respect.

I guess I wanted that, too. I just didn't think it was worth the lengths she would go to to get it. And none of them really worked. Until the Pill.

So Mom signed up like she always did, putting the meetings and dosage times on the calendar. Dad rolled his eyes and said he hoped this time didn't end with her crying about not being able to take a shit again. He met my eyes behind her back and we both smiled.

She just clucked her tongue at him. "Your language, Carl, honestly. You've been out of the navy a long time."

Dad tapped his pad and put in time to meet with his D&D buddies while Mom was busy with this new trial group. I smiled a little. I was glad he was going to do something fun. He had seemed pretty down lately. I was going to be busy, too. I had Visionaries, my school's filmmaking club. We had shoots set up every night for two weeks, trying to make this gonzo horror movie about a virus that turned the football team into cannibals. (Look, I didn't write it. I was the director of photography.)

Off Mom went to eat pills and answer questions about her habits. I had heard her go through all of this before and learned to hold my tongue. But I knew exactly how it would go: Mom would sit primly in a chair in a nice outfit, trying to cross her legs and never being able to hold that position. Her thighs would spread out on top of one another and slowly slide apart, seeking the space to sag around the arms of the chair and make her seem wider than ever, like a water balloon pooling on a hot sidewalk. She would never tell the whole truth. It was maybe the thing I hated about her the most.

"Oh yes, I exercise every day!"

She walked about twenty minutes a day total, from her car to her office and back again. Her treadmill was covered in clothes on hangers, and her dumbbells were fuzzed with a mortar made of dust and cat hair.

"I try to eat right, but I have bad habits that stem from stress."

Rain or shine, good day or bad, Mom had three scoops of ice cream with caramel sauce every night at ten.

"I do think I come by it honestly. My parents were both heavy. And my sisters and most of my cousins, too."

That one's true. The whole family is fat. In our last family photo, we wore an assortment of bright-colored shirts and we looked like a basket of round, ripe fruit. I kind of liked it, but I think I might have been the only one. The composition of the shots was good, and we all looked happy. Happy wasn't enough, apparently. Mom paid for those, but she never hung them up.

She came home from the first few sessions chatty and keyed up. She posted on her timelines how happy she was to be trying something really innovative and how she had a good feeling about this one. She wasn't allowed to say much; they made her sign an NDA. Later, I think she was glad that nobody could ask her the details.

I knew this time was going to be different the first night I heard the screaming. I had been up way past midnight, trying to edit footage of football players lumbering, meat-crazed, hands outstretched against the outline of the goalposts in a sunset-orange sky. My eyes had gotten hot and I'd had to put two icepacks under my laptop to cool down the CPU. (The machine just wasn't up to all that processing and rendering.) I woke up at four to the sound of it, jolting upright, my heart in my ears like someone had stuffed a tiny drum set into my head. I was so tired and out of it, I almost didn't know what I was hearing. But it was her voice. Mom was screaming like she was on fire. She did it so long and loud and unbroken that I couldn't understand how she could get her breath at all. It was out, out, out, and hardly a gasp in.

I ran into the hallway and smacked straight in Andrew, who was going the same way. We whacked belly against belly and fell backward on our butts like a couple of cartoon characters. I can picture it exactly in my head and imagine the way I'd frame it, the sound effects we could layer over the top. But in the moment, there was no time to laugh or argue. We just scrambled back up and made for our parents' bedroom door.

It was locked.

"Dad!" I hammered my fist against the hollow-core six-panel barrier. "Dad, what's happening? Is Mom OK?"

There was an unintelligible string of sounds from him. With Mom screaming like a steam whistle, there was no chance to make it out.

"I'm calling 911," Andrew yelled. His phone was already in his hand.

When the door opened, the sound of Mom's screaming hit us at full force, and Andrew and I both stumbled backward a little. The door had muffled it only slightly, but when the sound is your own mother dying, a little counts for a lot.

Dad was there, his gray hair a mess that pointed fingers in every direction, seeming to blame everyone at once. He put a hand out to Andrew, his face in a grimace, his eyes wide.

"Don't. Don't call anyone. Your mother says this is part of the trial she's in. She said it's worse than she thought it would be, but it only lasts for fifteen minutes."

Andrew looked at his phone. "I woke up almost ten minutes ago, when she was just growling."

"Growling," I asked. "What?"

Andrew rolled his eyes. "You could sleep through a nuclear strike."

Dad was nodding, looking at his watch. "We're almost out of it. Just hold on."

"Dad," Andrew said, "the neighbors probably already called the cops. She's really loud."

Dad's grimace widened. "I'm going to have to—"

The screaming stopped. The three of us looked at each other.

"Carl?" Mom's voice sounded exhausted and raw.

Dad fixed us both with a stern look, oscillating between the two of us. "You two don't call anyone. You don't tell anyone. Your mother is entitled to a little privacy. Is that understood?"

We looked at each other and said nothing.

Mom called again and he was gone, back on the other side of the door.

I didn't go back to sleep. I'm betting Andrew didn't either. But we stayed in our rooms for the next three hours, until it was time for breakfast. I went back to editing footage, and I was pretty pleased with what I'd be able to show to the Visionaries the next day. The movie was going to come in on schedule. It was great to have a project, something to take my mind off the weirdness in the night. I'm betting Andrew just signed on to his game. That's all he ever does.

I heard him turn off his alarm on the other side of the wall, followed by the sound of him standing up out of his busted computer chair with a grunt. He's way fatter than me, so I feel like I'm allowed to be disgusted by some of his habits. Andrew can't sit or stand without making a guttural, bovine noise. I've seen crumbs trapped in the folds of his neck. I used to work really hard to not be one of Those Fat People. I was obsessively clean, took impeccable care of my skin. I never showed my upper arms or my thighs, no matter what the occasion. I acted like being fat was impolite, like burping, and the best thing to do was conceal it behind the back of my hand and then always, always beg somebody's pardon.

I didn't know anything back then.

Andrew made it to the stairs before I did, so I got to watch him jiggle and shuffle down them, filled with loathing and disgust. I couldn't remember what bullshit diet we were supposed to be following that week, but I vowed to myself that no matter how small breakfast was, I would eat less of it than Andrew. I would leave something behind on the plate. Let Andrew be the one to lick his fingers and whine. I was above all that. Wheat toast and cut apples were waiting for us when we came into the kitchen.

And there was Mom at the coffee pot, fifty pounds lighter. Her pajamas hung off her like a hand-me-down from a much bigger sister. She turned, cup in hand, and I saw the dark circles beneath her eyes. She was beaming, however, with the biggest smile I'd seen on her face in years.

"It's working," she said, her voice still rough and edged with fatigue like she'd been to a rock concert or an all-night bonfire. "This thing is actually working."

That was our life for two weeks. Dad did his best to soundproof their bathroom. He stapled carpets and foam and egg crate to the walls. He covered the floor in a dozen fluffy bath mats he bought cheaply on the internet. He told me later that he tried to put a rag in her mouth, just to muffle her a little more.

"But I'm worried she'll pull it into her throat and choke on it," he told me, his eyes wide with dread. "I can't stand this much longer. I know she's losing weight, but it's like I'm living in a nightmare and I can't wake up."

That was a year before he decided to take the Pill, and back then he was more willing to talk about it. When it wasn't his own privacy, only hers, he would tell me how gross it was. You can see videos of it online. It was the same in that first trial as it is now: you take the Pill and you shit out your fat cells. In huge, yellow, unmanageable flows at first. That's why they scream so much. Imagine shitting fifty pounds of yourself at a go. Now, people go to special spas where they have crematoiletaries that burn the fat down. Dad said Mom screwed up our plumbing so bad that he had to buy a whole case of that lye-based stuff to break it all down and keep the toilet flushing. That was as gross as I thought things could get, but Dad said it got worse.

Toward the end, Mom (and everyone like her) shit out all their extra skin, too. The process that broke it down meant no stretch marks and no baggy leftovers, hanging on your body like overproofed dough on a hook and telling people you used to be fat.

That was some trick, and it was part of the reason it took so long for a generic to hit the market. It was a "trade secret," they said on the news. They also said "miracle" and "breakthrough" and "historic." The miracle of shitting out skin just looked like blood and collagen and rotten meat, it turns out. Not less gross, but different. More lye into the S bend. More and more of Mom gone at the breakfast table.

At the end of the trial, she was a person I didn't recognize. She was 110 lb. soaking wet. The research doctor told her that she was at 18 percent body fat and would stay that way for the rest of her life. Her face was a whole new shape, with the underlying structure very prominent and her eyes huge and wide above it all. I could see her hip bones beneath her enormous drawstring pants, pulled tight as a laundry bag around her now-tiny waist. Her collarbones could have held up a taco each. The cords in her neck stood out like chicken bones caught under her skin. Even her feet were smaller—she went down one whole shoe size, and I inherited all her stretched-out sandals and sneakers.

I slid my feet into them, thinking how it was like my mom had died and some other woman had moved in. Late at night, I gathered up all the clothes she had given me and bundled them into the garbage. They were ugly, but they also felt somehow humiliating to wear. I couldn't explain the impulse. Luckily, she never asked me where any of it went. She was very focused on herself in those days.

"It finally happened," Mom told me with tears in her eyes. "They finally made a Pill that gives you the perfect body, no matter what."

And yeah, she could eat anything she wanted and didn't have to work out. As long as she kept taking the small maintenance dose of the Pill, she would stay this way for as long as she lived. Which she thought would be much longer, now that she didn't have to carry around the threats of diabetes and heart disease everywhere she went.

I remember one day I walked in and found her and Dad sitting at the kitchen table, both of them obviously crying. They tried to hide it from me; Dad ducked his face into the shawl collar of his sweater, Mom swiping her eyes with quick fingers.

"What's up with you guys?" I asked, trying not to look.

"Nothing, honey. There's carrot and celery sticks cut fresh and sitting in water in the fridge, if you want a snack."

Mom's voice was thick in her throat; she'd really been sobbing.

I ignored both the sorrow and the content of what she'd said and fished around in the cabinet over the sink until I found one individually wrapped chocolate cupcake.

"I'm good," I said and tried to leave the kitchen.

"Honey, do you think I lost all this weight so that I could leave you guys?"

I stopped and turned on the spot like something on a rotating plate, a pizza in a microwave. I couldn't help it. I should have just kept walking.

"What?"

Dad buried his face some more. Mom just looked at me, her eyes all shiny. "Did you ever think that my desire to lose weight was about you? Like, do you feel like I'm trying to leave you behind?"

I stared at her. There wasn't anything I could say. How could I feel any other way? How did she not know how obvious she was? Every diet, every scheme, every study was just her trying to find a way out of being what we are. Every time she tried to change who she was, who we all were, it was like betrayal.

I looked over at Dad and realized this wasn't about me. He was worried she was going to *physically* leave him, now that she thought she was hot enough to hook up with somebody else. I saw it all at once: the way she was never worried about me being on birth control, the way Dad looked at other women in the supermarket. The way all of us were so focused on what we looked like, as if it mattered, as if being thin was the only kind of life worth living.

So I lied.

"No, Mom. I don't think about it at all, I guess. It really has nothing to do with me."

I left them alone and went to eat my cupcake in peace. I looked at the timer I'd had running on my phone since the beginning of junior year: the countdown to the day I'd leave for college. I wanted out even then, but I hadn't sent out applications yet. Back then, two years seemed like forever.

Mom and Dad made up, I guess. They never told us anything that mattered. Anyway, that was when the deaths started to make the news.

The averages are still debated all the time, because preexisting conditions can't be ruled out. But people seem to agree it's about one in ten. In each group of thirty participants in the early studies, ten were control, ten got the placebo, and the final ten got the Pill. Nine out of ten shit themselves to perfection. That tenth one, though. They ended up slumped on a toilet, blood vessels burst in their eyes, hearts blown out by the strain of converting hundreds of pounds of body mass to waste.

I never thought it would get approved with a 10 percent fatality rate, but I guess I was really naive. The truth was it got fast-tracked and approved by the FDA within a year. Mom was in a commercial, talking about how it gave her her life back, but this was a life she had never had. It gave her someone else's life entirely. Some life she had never even planned for. In the commercial, she wore a teal sports bra and a lot of makeup. I did not recognize her at all. She stood next to that celebrity, the one who did it first. What's her name—Amy Blanton.

Remember those ads? "Get the Amy Blanton body!" She had gained a little weight after she had her kids, but her Before picture and Mom's Before picture looked like members of two different species. In the commercial, their former selves got *whisked* away, and there they were: exactly the same height, exactly the same build. A little contouring and a blowout made them twins. Mom had the Amy Blanton body. For just a little while, people would stop her on the street and ask if she *was* Amy Blanton. That got old fast. I used to just walk away fatly while she pretended she looked nothing like her TV twin.

I watched Dad grow more and more insecure about the change in Mom. I saw him get mad at a guy at the gas station who checked out Mom's ass when she bent over.

"Get back in the car, Carl. Gosh, you're making a scene about nothing. It was just a compliment!"

Dad sat down, fuming, but he wouldn't close his door. His ears were bright red. Andrew was playing a game on his phone, totally zoned out. I watched Dad trying to calm himself down.

"You probably haven't been jealous about Mom since you guys were kids, huh?"

He blew out hot air through his nose like a bull. "Try *ever*," he said, his voice tight.

"Wasn't Mom hot as a teenager?"

His lips closed into a line I could see in the rearview mirror. "She was always heavy. She was . . . she was *mine*, god damnit."

That sort of shocked me. He hadn't ever talked about her that way before. And it hadn't ever occurred to me that maybe my dad the football player had gotten with my less-than-perfect mom because he knew she'd never cheat on him. Could never. Just like she thought I could never go out and get myself in trouble. Because fat girls don't fuck, I guess?

I looked over at Andrew, too big for a seatbelt, pooling against the car door. Did fat boys fuck? Was anybody going to pick him because he'd be *theirs*? I didn't want to imagine. But just as I was feeling sorry for us all, Mom slid lithely back into the car.

"Don't be a goose, honey," she said. She laid a hand on Dad's knee. "You have nothing to worry about."

That turned out to be a lie.

It was about a month after FDA approval when Dad announced to us that he was gonna take the Pill.

I couldn't help but give Mom the look of death. He'd never have done it if she hadn't gone first and made him worry about losing her. Andrew grunted at the news the way he grunted at everything, as if nothing in the world held much interest for him.

I hate crying, but I burst into tears. I couldn't even yell at Mom. I just wanted to talk Dad out of it. I tried for weeks, and I ended up trying again on the day he began treatment. I just had this feeling in my gut that he was going to be one of the unlucky ones.

"One in ten," I croaked at him, my voice wrecked by crying. "One in *ten*, Dad. It's just slightly better odds than Russian roulette."

He smiled from his spa-hospital bed with the special trench installed below. He was wearing one of those paper gowns, and I thought how stupid he would feel dying in paper clothes while taking a shit. Was it worth it? How could it be worth it?

"But the odds of dying young if I stay fat are much worse," he told me in his sweet voice. He reached out and put a hand on my shoulder, and I heard his gown rustling like trash dragging through the gutter when it's windy. "Don't worry, Munchkin. It's in god's hands."

I guess it was, but I had never trusted god not to drop stuff and break it.

Dad made it to the third treatment. It felt cruel, like I had just started to relax and believe that he might be OK.

We came back and saw him on day one, down about fifty pounds and looking like someone had slapped him around all night.

"Honey, you look wonderful," Mom cooed, kissing his cheeks and hugging him to her middle. Andrew had stayed home. I looked him up and down, remembering the way Mom had just melted to reveal the stranger within.

"You look OK," I managed to say.

"I told you, kiddo." We sat with him while he ate some graham crackers and drank lots of water. My parents held hands.

I skipped the second visit. The knots in my stomach were huge and twisting, and I just couldn't face it. Mom came home whistling and very pleased with herself.

"He's in the home stretch now! I can't wait for you kids to see what your Dad really looks like."

I just sat there, wondering if I was real. Are fat people fake? Do we not have souls? Does nothing I do count if I do it while I'm fat? These were questions I had never really thought about before, but with both of my parents risking death to be less like me, I suddenly had to wonder about a lot of things.

I knew the minute Mom picked up the phone the next day. I could tell she wasn't expecting the call. She stared at it just a second too long before she picked it up. My film professor calls that a beat, like a drumbeat or a heartbeat. One beat too many, and I knew.

One beat too many and Dad's heart gave in.

Neither one of us could go with Mom to deal with the body. Andrew wouldn't even leave his room. I don't remember those weeks very clearly. I remember weird parts.

Mom buying Dad a new suit he could be buried in, because nothing he owned would fit. Mom saying Dad wouldn't want to be cremated, now that he was thin. Dad's D&D buddies looking into his casket and saying how great he looked. The never-ending grief buffet of casseroles and cake in our kitchen. The nights when I could hear Mom crying through the vents.

That should have been the last of it. Other people could die, even famous people, but the Pill killed my Dad. That should have been it, end of story, illegal forever. But that's not how anything works. The world is just allowed to wound you any way it wants and move on.

And so are the people you know.

The minute Andrew brought it up, I almost laughed. There was no way Mom was going to let him do it, after what had happened to Dad. Maybe we weren't the best of buds, but I didn't want him to die.

I could hear her in his room, and she was never in his room. It was permadark in there, blackout shades on the windows and nothing but the dim blue glow of his monitors to light it. I could hear them talking and I came close to the door, not quite putting my ear to it.

"I'm too old to be on your insurance," he said. "But they're saying there's gonna be a generic within a year, so it'll probably be cheaper."

"I think that's the best idea, sweetheart. But you're still going to have to pay for your hospital stay. We have a little money from Dad's insurance, so I can help you with that. It's what your father would have wanted."

I pushed the door open, already yelling. "No. No. No. No. It is not what Dad would have wanted. Dad would have wanted to be alive. Do you want to end up dead, too?"

They both stared at me like I had come through the door on fire.

"What is the matter with you?"

"Yeah," Andrew sneered. "Don't you knock?"

Mom put her hands on her hips. "This is a private conversation, kiddo."

"I don't give a shit," I told them. "We just buried our dad, and you want to take the Pill that killed him. How stupid can you be?"

Andrew shrugged. "Ninety percent is still an A."

"And dead is still dead," I said at once. "There's no curve on that."

Mom came and took my elbow and walked me back toward the door. "You're letting your emotions get the best of you," she said. I could hear her voice trembling, and when I looked up her eyes were wet in the dim blue light of the bedroom. "I miss him too, but I don't let it cloud my judgment. Your brother needs to do what's best for him."

"It's better for him to be dead than fat," I shot back. "Is that really what you think?"

We both turned back to look at Andrew.

Andrew would never tell me his actual weight, but I had heard him say once that he was in the "five club." Nothing fit him but the absolute biggest shirts and elastic waistband shorts, and he wouldn't wear shoes that had to be tied. His fingers were so fat he could barely use his phone and finally upgraded to one with a stylus.

He sighed at us both. "I'm tired of this," he said to me, but Mom started to cry. "I'm tired of never going out and never fitting in a chair. I'm tired of getting stared at and having to hide from people to eat. Aren't you tired of it, sis?"

I shrugged. "I'm not tired of being alive."

I didn't convince him. I didn't convince Mom. She gave him the money and he checked himself in. I went with them, only because I was worried I wouldn't get to say goodbye otherwise.

Andrew was twenty-four when he did it, and his doctor had to get his digs in first. I remember his old-man chuckle as he lined my brother up next to the chart on the wall. "Well, son. You're not going to get any taller. And let's quit getting wider while we can, shall we?"

Andrew laughed with him, as if his fat self was already somebody else. Someone who it was OK to laugh at. My thin Mom laughed, too. Somewhere in thin heaven, was Dad laughing? Already I was an anomaly on the streets. I'm sure it used to be hard to be fat in LA or New York. I've read about that. But living in Dayton, Ohio, meant always fitting in the booth at a restaurant and never being the only fat person in the room. By the time Andrew got the Pill, I couldn't count on those things anymore. A year later, the whole world was shrinking around me, and I could already feel the pinch.

Andrew came home from the hospital looking like some other guy; a dude who played basketball and got called Slim. His eyes were bright.

"Munchkin, I can't wait for you to do it. It's amazing! I mean, it's super gross and really painful, but after that it's the fucking awesomest."

They had all called me Munchkin since I was a kid. Not because I was short and cute, but because they said I was always munching. I hated that nickname and he knew it. He was just using it now to remind me I was the only one left.

"You look like Dad looked in his casket," I said.

He tried for a little while to go out and enjoy his new thin life, but he didn't really know how. He couldn't talk to anybody. He missed his online friends and he hated the sunlight, the noise, the feeling of people always around, sizing him up. He had a new body, but it didn't matter.

I watched Andrew go back to this gaming pod; the ruined chair with the cracked spar he had fixed with duct tape no longer sagging or groaning beneath him. The same shiny spots on his computer where he kept his hands in the same positions for fourteen hours at a time while he pretended he was a tall, muscular Viking warrior on some Korean server every day. I watched him settle right back into his old life using his new body and wondered what it was for. He really was the Viking now. He could have put on boots and left the house and had a real adventure. But adventure didn't appeal to him.

I was stuck between them in the house. I always had been, but Dad and I had understood each other. We had been a team. I guess I was a daddy's girl, but I was never spoiled like that. We just got along. Andrew was silent and Mom never shut up. Dad was the only one I could talk to, or sit in silence with without feeling bad.

And now I was the only fat member of the family. Slowly but surely, even the aunts and cousins signed up to take the Pill. I started to joke with my friends in Visionaries that fat people were going to become an endangered species.

Some of them laughed, but a couple suggested we actually make a short film about that. We kicked the idea around, but mostly they wanted to film me eating in a cage while people stared. I didn't know how that would get anything meaningful across, and they didn't know how not to be thin assholes. So we dropped the idea.

Mom was at least using the way she had changed to enjoy the real world a little more. She wore workout clothes constantly, all bright colors and cling like the patterning on a snake. Every day she got to enjoy the way people looked at her brightly now, eyebrows up, not searching for their first chance to sidle away.

"People just respond to me so much better now," she said in one of her interviews. "It changes everything about my daily interactions. I'm a mother and a widow, and I don't need a lot of attention," she had said, smiling coyly. "But even the mailman is happier to see me than he ever was before."

I wanted to barf when she said she didn't need attention. She had been thirsty enough before to talk to absolutely anyone, even sign up to take injections and hypnosis to get it. Now she was always posing and watching to see who would look. Attention was like the drug she couldn't get enough of. She still ate the same bowl of ice cream every night, sitting next to the groove in the couch where Dad used to fit. No, Mom, you didn't need attention. You took the Pill, you let the Pill take Dad because you were so A-OK with yourself.

The Pill sold like nothing had ever sold before. The original, the generic, the knockoffs, the different versions approved in Europe and Asia that met their standards and got rammed through their testing. There was at last a cure for the obesity epidemic. Fat people really were an endangered species. And everybody was so, so glad.

One in ten kept dying. The average never improved, not in any corner of the globe. There were memorials for the famous and semifamous folks who took the gamble and lost. A congressman here and a comedian there. But everyone was so proud of them that they had died trying to better themselves that all the obituaries and eulogies had a weird, wistful tone to them. As if it was the next best thing to being thin. At least they didn't have to live that fat life anymore.

And every time it was on the news, we sat in silence and didn't talk about Dad.

I was just a kid when Mom made it through the original trial that unleashed the Pill on the world. It wasn't approved for teenagers, not anywhere. Don't get me wrong; teens and parents alike were more than ready to sign up for the one-in-ten odds of dying. But the scientists who had worked on the Pill said unequivocally that it should not be taken by anyone who was not absolutely done growing. Eighteen was the minimum, but they recommended twenty-one to be completely safe.

On my eighteenth birthday, my mom threw me a party. She invited all my friends (mostly the Visionaries) and decorated the backyard with yellow roses and balloons.

It was the first time since Dad died that the house seemed cheerful. Mom ordered this huge lemon cake at the good bakery, with layers of custard filling and sliced strawberries. I remember everybody moaning over how good it was, how summery-sweet. People danced, but I felt too self-conscious to get up and give it a try. My mom ended up dancing with a neighbor who heard the music and came through the gate to check it out. He was skinny, too, and I couldn't watch them together.

We ate barbecue ribs and I got to tell people over and over again where I'd gotten into college. Northwestern. Rutgers. Cornell. And UCLA. Where was I going to go? Oh, I hadn't decided yet, but I needed to pick soon.

Except I definitely had. I had wanted to study filmmaking my whole life. Everybody in the Visionaries club knew that; they had all applied to UCLA and USC. A few of us got in. It wasn't just that it was my dream school in the golden city where movies were made. It was also about as far away as I could get. Mom reminded me that I could go anywhere in-state for free because of her job, saying it over and over with that look in her eye, the one that said *don't leave me*, but I was going to LA if I had to walk every mile.

When it came time for presents, I got some jewelry from my grandmother. She didn't come and I couldn't blame her; she was my dad's mom. A lace parasol from my friends, who all expected I'd need protection from the sun sometime soon. Books and music and a clever coffee cup. A fountain pen. The kinds of things that signal adulthood is about to begin.

My mom, beaming, gave me the Pill.

"I can't give you the physical thing, of course," she said, glancing around for a laugh. She got a little one. She handed me her iPad. "This has all of the paperwork, showing that you've been approved and my insurance will cover it. Plus, I booked your spa stay so that you'll have time to buy all new clothes before leaving for school." She smiled like she'd never killed my dad.

"I don't . . . know what to say," I said finally. If I said what I was actually feeling, it might mean she wouldn't pay for school, I'd be on my own. I had to swallow it. But I'd be damned if I was gonna swallow that Pill.

The party broke up slowly, with the neighbor guy hanging around and trying to talk to Mom until she texted Andrew and made him come down and walk the guy out. I packed up all my presents. I thanked Mom as sincerely as I could. I wrapped up slices of cake for people who wanted to take them home. And I seethed.

I left for UCLA two weeks early. I told Mom I was planning to come back and take my medicine over Thanksgiving break. She said she understood my delay, that I was just worried I'd pull the short straw and that it was OK to be nervous. She put me on the plane to Los Angeles with tears in her eyes.

On the flight, it was me and one other fat kid, maybe ten years old. That was it. The woman who sat next to me huffed and whined about it until the flight attendant brought her a free drink to shut her up. It was the first time I had ever been on a plane, and I sat there wondering whether it was always as uncomfortable as this. I could see the other fat kid up a few rows, hanging his elbow and one knee into the aisle. He wasn't even full-grown and already he was too big for an airplane seat. I wished we had been sitting together. We would have recognized each other. It would have been like having family again. Everyone else had that same Pill body.

And it was always the exact same body. No more thick thighs or really round asses. No more wide tits or pointy pecs or love handles rounding out someone's sides. Everyone's body was flat planes and straight lines. It wasn't just that they were thin. They were all somehow the same.

In LA the change was striking. I had heard that even thin people were taking the Pill out there to ensure that they'd never gain any weight, but I didn't believe it until I started seeing the change on TV and in movies. One by one, distinctive shapes disappeared. It was always the Amy Blanton body, like my mom had. The guys all had the same Ethan Fairbanks body. He once did a bunch of ads with some nobody. Only faces and hair color, a little difference in height could distinguish one actor from another. Here and there, a death. Worth it, everyone whispered like a prayer. Worth it, worth it, worth it.

I made it a few months at UCLA. My classes were cool and I started to make friends right off. But little things kept piling up. I went to the student store to buy myself a UCLA hoodie and they had nothing that would fit me. It wasn't even close. I looked at the largest size in the men's section and even then it would have clung to me like the skin of a sausage. I decided I could live without that ubiquitous symbol of college life, but I was pissed. I even thought about buying one just to snip the logo out and sew it onto a hoodie in my size from Walmart.

Then Walmart stopped carrying plus sizes altogether.

There were no desks on campus that I could sit at. A few of the classrooms had long tables with detached chairs and those were all right. But the majority of my freshman classes were in those big lecture halls, with the rows and rows of wooden chair-and-desk combinations. I couldn't wedge myself into one to save my life. My first or second day I tried really hard in the back row and just got a big bruise over my lowest rib for my troubles. I sat in the aisle, on the steps, or against the back wall every day. There just wasn't any space for me.

My dorm room was the same way. The bed was narrow and I could hear the whole frame groaning the second I lay down. The bathroom was so small that I could touch both walls with my thighs when I sat on the toilet. My roommate was so thin I knew she hadn't taken the Pill—she still looked too original. But over the course of the first week, I realized that was because she never ate. I asked her to lunch a couple of times, but she always said no. I couldn't save her. I was working on how to save myself.

Days ticked by and Thanksgiving break was bearing down on me. My mom kept calling, telling me how great it was going to be when I went back to the school in my ideal body.

"I don't know that it'll be my ideal body," I told her. "It'll just be different."

"Don't you want to go on dates like the other girls?" Her voice was so whiny I could barely stand it.

I looked across the room to the other girl I lived with. She was in her bra, and every time she breathed in I could see the impressions of her individual ribs against the skin of her back. She was doing her reading and sucking on her bottom lip as if her lip gloss might offer some calories.

"I don't know that I want anything other girls have," I told her. But that wasn't true. Most girls had fathers.

"You don't know what you're missing," Mom said. "Come on home and let's get you squared away."

"Soon," I told her, counting the days until I had to let them try to kill me for being what I am.

I had been there about a month when I knew I wasn't going to make it. The stares had become unmanageable. I wasn't the last fat girl in LA, was I? People on campus avoided me like I was a radioactive werewolf who stank like a dead cat in a hot garage. I remember one time I tried to take a selfie to send home to the Visionaries and someone gasped out loud. In the picture, I could see him, mouth open like he'd glimpsed a ghost.

And in a way I guess I was. I was the ghost of fatness past, haunting the open breezeways of UCLA. I was what they used to be, what they had always feared they would become. I became obsessed with the terrible power of my fatness; I was the worst that could possibly happen to someone. Worse than death, had to be, because somewhere my dad was rotting in a box because that was easier than living in a body like mine. I knew when I frightened people and I pushed my advantage. I took up their space. I haunted them with my warm breath and my soft elbows. I fed on their fright.

It was early November, and I could not adjust to the lack of seasons. It was still warm and sunny like June on the California coast. I missed home, but the idea of home repelled me. I needed comfort.

I walked myself over to the cheap pancake house and ordered the never-ending stack and coffee. The all-you-can-eat pancake special was always a favorite with frat boys, and its popularity had only increased since the Pill hit the market. People who really loved to eat could finally do it without worrying that it would ruin their lives.

The hostess tried to seat me in a booth and I just rolled my eyes at her. I was not about to eat my weight in pancakes with a formica tabletop wedged just beneath my sternum.

"A table, please."

She stuck me in the back, next to the restrooms. I didn't care.

My first four pancakes showed up hot and perfect and I asked for extra butter. When they were just right (dripping, not soaked and turning into paste) I shoveled up huge bites into my waiting mouth, letting it fill me as nothing else did. Who could care that they were the last of their kind when the zoo had such good food?

And yeah, people were staring. People are always staring at me. That was a constant of my existence, and I was used to it. I ignored them. I slurped up hot coffee and wiped the plate down with the last bite of cake.

"Hit me again," I said, and the waitress took the plate away. A few minutes later, another fresh hot stack of pancakes appeared.

I didn't know how many times I could do it, but that was the day I was going to find out.

And then a man sat at my table.

He was perfectly ordinary, with brown hair and brown eyes. He had the Pill body underneath his tan suit. I looked him over.

"Can I help you?"

He stared at my mouth for a minute and I waited. "Do you have any idea how beautiful you are?" he finally asked.

I rolled my eyes hard and started to butter my pancakes. I was going to need more butter. "Fuck off, creep."

He put a hand against his own chest. "Please, I meant no disrespect. I'm being sincere. You're so lovely. So rare. I haven't seen a woman like you in almost a year."

I waved to the waitress but she didn't see me. I debated. I'd rather have the butter, but if the cakes got cold before it showed up, it would hardly matter at all. I scraped the dish that I had and began to cut up pancakes and ignore my visiting weirdo, hoping he would go away.

He cleared his throat and ordered a cup of coffee. "Please, allow me to entertain you while you eat and I'll pick up your check."

I sighed. Few things were as motivating as free food. So I let him sit.

He asked me about cinematography, about why I had come to LA. I talked in between cups of coffee and plates of pancakes.

"I had all these ideas about the story only I could tell when I got here. The things that were unique to my experience. It's funny now, because there was nothing unique about my experience. I guess everybody thinks they're one of a kind."

He glanced over his shoulder a little, then pushed the cream pitcher toward me for my coffee. "Look around. You nearly are."

I shrugged. "I guess. But there's no way to tell this story so that people will understand it. You ever see the way fat people on the street are shot for news stories? Headless and limbless and wide as the world, always wandering like they've got nowhere to be. That's the only story people know. We were always a joke, we were always invisible. And now, we're going to disappear. Because we were never meant to exist in the first place."

"Are you?" he asked, cocking an eyebrow. "Going to disappear?"

"Who the hell are you?" I finally asked.

He sighed and finished his coffee. "I can't tell you that. But I can show you something that might change your mind."

I don't know why I said yes. Maybe I was dreading going back to school where nothing fit. Maybe I just didn't want to answer the question of whether I was going to take the Pill. Maybe it was just the way he looked at me—really looked at me. Not like I was a problem to be solved or some walking glitch in the way things are supposed to work.

I got into a strange man's car outside of the pancake house and I let him show me.

The club was up in the hills, just off Mulholland Drive. It was in this gorgeous house, built in the golden age of Hollywood for some chiseled hunk who had died of AIDS. The lawn was perfect and I could smell the chlorine in the pool the minute I stepped out of the car. The neighborhood was the kind of quiet where you know that even the gardeners muffle their equipment.

My nameless escort walked up the stone path toward a wide, shaded, black front door. He looked back over his shoulder, glancing at me.

"You coming?"

I was.

It was dark inside the house at first, my eyes adjusting from the bright sunshine slowly. After a few minutes, I saw that it was merely dim. The living room was furnished beautifully, sumptuously, with a clear emphasis on texture and deep padding. The room was empty except for one woman, sitting on a chaise longue and reading a book.

We approached her and she looked up. She was an absolute knockout: a redhead with full lips and built like an hourglass that had time to spare. Her dress clung to her, making a clear case that she enjoyed being looked at. She was not walking around in an Amy Blanton body. She was an original.

The man I came in with tapped his fingers on the top of her book and said, "In the chocolate war, I fought on the side of General Augustus."

The redhead nodded, not saying a word. She shifted in her seat and reached for something I couldn't see. Behind her, a bookshelf slid sideways, revealing a deep purple tunnel behind it.

I nodded to her as we passed, and she smiled at me with a hunger I couldn't put a name to. I had no idea where we were headed.

We walked through a series of rooms. The entire house was decorated in the same style as that first room: sensual, decadent, and plush. As I got to see more of it, I realized that everything was also built wide, sturdy, and I'd never think twice about sitting in any chair I saw.

In every room I passed, I saw the same thing as I peered through the door. There was a fat person surrounded by thin people staring at them. Some of the onlookers were crying, some were visibly aroused. Different races, different genders. All well-dressed. All nearly identical in those Pill bodies. A tall fat woman was lounging, shrouded by veils in a Turkish bed, nude and lolling and made of endless undulations of honey-colored flesh. She fed herself grapes while someone was making her laugh. Ten people sat around her bed, watching.

A fat man, as big as Andrew used to be, was dipping his gloved fists into paint and punching a blank, white wall. He was being videotaped and photographed, lit gorgeously while people murmured praise and encouragements.

In one room, a short black woman whose curves defied gravity ran oil-slicked hands over her nudity, smiling a perfect, satisfied smile. Two men stood near her, their mouths open, hungering endlessly, asking nothing of her.

We came to an empty room that had a round tub at its end and a set of low stone benches. The domed ceiling made our footfalls sound epic. The water had steam rising off it, even in the warmth of the house, and smelled like the sea.

"Salt water," he said. "Much better for your skin. Would you like to take a dip? You don't have to talk to anyone or do anything, but some people may come join you. How does that sound?"

"I don't have a bathing suit."

His smile was slow and he dropped his chin like he was about to share a conspiracy. "Have you looked around? Nobody will mind."

"What are these people getting out of this? I don't need this."

He pulled out his phone and showed me the app that the house used to keep track of money. Each fat performer had an anonymous identifier and a live count of what they were making.

"Maybe I could persuade you to work for a couple of hours, just to see what you think? You'll make the house minimum, plus tips."

I watched the numbers climb up. "Just to sit here? I don't have to touch anybody? Or even make conversation?"

He nodded. "We'd prefer that you work in the nude, but you don't even have to do that. Just enjoy the hot soak. What do you say?"

It sounded weird as fuck, but I wanted two things immediately. First, I wanted the money. If I was going to go home and refuse the Pill, I was pretty sure I was going to need it. Second, I wanted to go back to the room where the boxing painter was being filmed. I itched to get behind a camera in this place, to tell the story of the endangered species of fat people. Not like the Visionaries had wanted it, but the way I wanted it. Like this. Dark and rich and seductive.

I got into the water in my bra and panties. I may as well have gotten naked; they were both white cotton and went see-through in the water. I tried not to think about it. I dunked my head, sat on one of the submerged steps, and soaked with my neck laid back against the rim.

I could hear people coming and going. I could hear the things they whispered to me. Voices in the salty dark called me rare and magnificent and soft and enticing. I said nothing. I didn't even hint that I could hear.

After a few hours, my nameless handler came back with a fluffy, soft towel the size of a bedsheet that smelled like lavender. He thanked me and showed me how to download the app to get paid.

I had been there for three hours, and I had more money than I had ever had at one time, in my entire life. He watched my face very closely when I saw the number.

"My name's Dan," he said softly.

"Do you own this place?"

"No, I'm just a recruiter. I'm going to give you my number."

I watched him type it into my phone as "Dan Chez Corps."

"What makes you think I'll call you?"

I thought he was going to remind me of how much money I had just made, but he didn't. He kinda shook his head a little, then asked, "Where else are you going to go?"

He had brought me replacements for my wet underthings, much nicer than the ones I was wearing. They were exquisite and well made and carried no tags.

"A gift from the house," he said, before leaving me to change. They fit like they were made for me.

I went back to the dorm and watched my roommate twitch in her sleep. Her side of the fridge held a single hard-boiled egg and a pint of skim milk. My bed groaned beneath me as I lay down, still in my fancy gift underwear.

I dreamt about my dad.

The laws changed that year, but they wouldn't go into effect until January. They weren't making it illegal to be fat, exactly. But it was as close as they could get. It was going to be legal to deny health insurance to anyone with a BMI over 25 if they refused the Pill. Intentional obesity would also be grounds for loss of child custody and would be acceptable reason for dismissal from a job.

Where the law went, culture followed. Airlines were adding a customer weight limit and clothing manufacturers concentrated on developing lines to individualize the Pill body. Journalists wrote articles on the subject of renegade fats. Could their citizenship be revoked? Should parents of fat children be prosecuted for abuse if they didn't arrange for them to receive the Pill as soon as possible?

I submitted a treatment to my short film class detailing my desire to film a secret enclave where fat renegades performed for the gratification of a live Pilled audience. My professor wrote back to tell me that my idea was 1. obscene and 2. impossible.

The Friday before Thanksgiving break, Mom called.

"I'm so glad we're getting this done before the change in airline policy. Can you imagine having to come to Ohio by train? Anyhow, your Aunt Jeanne is coming in for the holiday—"

"Mom. Mom, listen. I don't want to do it."

"Do what? See Aunt Jeanne?"

"No, Mom, listen. I'm not going to take the Pill."

She was quiet for a minute. "Sweetie, we all took it hard when your father passed. I know you must be worried about that, but they say there's no genetic marker—"

"It's not just Dad. It's not just the odds that I might die. I just don't want to do it. I want to stay who I am."

She sighed like I was a child who had asked for the ninetieth time why the sky was blue. "This doesn't change who you are, Munchkin. It only changes your body."

"I'm not coming home," I said, flatly.

There was a lot of yelling, with both of us trying to be cruel to the other. I'd rather not remember it. What I do remember is her crying, saying something like, "I gave you your body. I made it, and it's imperfect like mine was. Why won't you let me fix it? Why won't you let me correct my mistake?"

"I don't feel like a mistake," I told her. "And I'm not coming home. Not now, not ever."

I remember hanging up and the terrible silence that followed. I remember thinking I should turn my phone off, but then I realized I could just leave it behind. I could leave everything behind. I took my camera and my laptop and left everything else. I didn't even take a change of clothes.

I borrowed a phone from someone on the quad, making up a story that mine had been stolen. She waited for me as I called Dan. I told him to pick me up where I was.

The car arrived ten minutes later.

The redhead buzzed me in without asking for a password, which was great because I couldn't remember what Dan had said.

Down through the purple hallway and a woman I'd never seen before shook my hand and told me I could call her Denny.

Denny had a Pill body, hidden away beneath a wide, flowing caftan and a matching headwrap. She showed me to my room, my king-size bed, my enormous private bath, my shared common room and library. She gave me the WiFi password and explained the house's security.

"You may stay here as long as you like. The house will feed you and clothe you. Your medical needs will be seen to. Your entertainments will be top-notch. You may leave anytime you wish. Your pay will be automatically deposited into your account as it comes in, without delay.

"However, you must never disclose the location or the nature of this house to anyone via any means; not by phone call or text or email. You may take photos and videos, but we have jammers to prevent geotagging of any kind. If you are found in violation of this one rule, you will walk out of here with nothing but the clothes on your back. Is that clear?"

I told her it was. She left and returned five minutes later with a new phone for me. I signed into my bank account—the one my mother wasn't on—and set about creating a new email, a new profile, a new identity.

I eased into the work. I ate cupcakes and I danced in a leotard. I read poetry aloud while sipping a milkshake. I lounged in a velvet chaise nude while people drew me and painted me. I began to speak to my admirers and I watched my pay skyrocket.

I met the house's head seamstress: a brilliant, nimble-fingered fat woman named Charisse. She had an incredible eye and hardly had to measure anyone. She made me corsets and skirts, silk pajamas and satin gowns, costumes and capes and all manner of underwear.

I realized when I had been wearing her work for months that some of my clothes were a little too small. My favorite bikini cut into me just so, just enough to accentuate the flesh it did not quite contain. I filmed myself in the hall of mirrors, wearing it and trying to understand what it meant.

Some of my gowns were a little too big, though I could remember the exactitude with which I was fitted. I made short clips showing the gaps in the waist and hips, the way I could work my whole hand in between the fabric and my skin.

Charisse was too skilled for it to be an accident. The implication became clear.

All around me there were heavenly bodies in gowns and togas, a stately fleet of well-rounded ships gliding alongside the pool or lying silkily in our beds. We were beautiful, but we were all aware of a subtle campaign to make us larger, ever larger, more suited to satisfy whatever it was that brought the throngs of thin whispering wantons to our door.

In twos and threes, we began to talk about what it meant. About who we could trust. About who was running this place, and why.

The lower floors of the house were a brothel. Somehow I knew that without being told. There was a look in the older fat folks' eyes that let me know it would be waiting for me when I was ready. Nobody pressured me. Nobody even asked. One day I just headed down the stairs. Cheeks were swabbed at the door and everybody waited fifteen minutes until they were cleared. I got my negatives and went through.

I'd never had sex before. I think it happens later for fat kids. While everyone else was trying each other on, I was still trying to figure out why I never fit into anything. I don't regret that. I can't imagine doing this out in the world where I am the worst thing that can happen to somebody.

I didn't know what it would be like. I hope it's this good for everyone, with a circle of adoring worshippers vying for the right to adore you, to touch every inch of you, to murmur in wonder as you climax again and again until nap time, when you are lovingly spooned and crooned to sleep. I luxuriated in it for a long time, not thinking about what it meant to only touch thin people, to only be touched by them. I watched my bank balance climb. I didn't ask myself what they saw when they looked at me. I existed as a collection of nerves that did not think.

I stopped thinking about going home. I stopped thinking about the Pill. I stopped thinking. I became what I had always been and nothing more: my fat, fat body.

When I came back to thinking again, I found it did not make things easier.

I have been here for three years now, and I don't think I can ever live anywhere else. Outside, they tell me, there are no more like me. Only in places like here, where a few of us fled before the world could change us. Nobody is allowed to bring us food presents anymore; everyone is too worried they'll try and slip us the Pill. Someone might actually be that upset that I exist. I don't think about that either. I don't exist for them. I accept their worship and forget their faces completely. It's always the same face anyhow.

Sometimes I point my camera at that face and ask them what they're doing here, what do they want, why did they come seeking the thing the thing they've worked so hard to avoid becoming?

They mumble about mothers and goddesses, about the embrace of flesh and the fullness of desire. It sounds like my own voice inside my head. I think about my dad, about god's hands. Would he have been one of these? Would he have come to miss my mother's body the way he first knew it?

I think about showing this film in LA. I think about Denny telling me I can leave here anytime. I think about how I could leave my body anytime, too, how any of us can. I think about Andrew, about how he left his and gained nothing at all. How I used to see him as the enemy when he was just me.

Deep down on the lowest floor, in perfect privacy, the fats make love to each other. There is a boy who came only a few weeks ago, an import from one of the countries that's taken to the Pill slowly, so we have a lot of recruits from their shores. We had no common language at first, but we've worked on that and discovered an unmapped country between us. He's so sweet and shy and eager to lift the heaviness of his belly so that he can slip inside me and then drop it on top of mine, warm and weighty like a curtain. He whispers to me that we don't ever have to go back, that we can raise darling fat babies right here, that we'll become like another species. *Homo pillus* can inherit the earth, while *Homo lipidus* lives in secret.

"But we'll live," he whispers to me as we conspire to remake the world in the image of our thick ankles. "We'll live," he says, his tongue tracing the salty trenches made by the folds in my sides. Belly to belly, fat against fat.

"We'll live."

Gone with *Gone with the Wind*

I AM A REREADER. I have been all my life. The habit was born of necessity: I grew up poor and itinerant. The books I accumulated were from thrift stores, picked up in paperback for fifty cents or in hardback for a lofty dollar. I tried to pick books that were long and would last me a while. Periods away from the library or school left me without fresh books, so I would read the good ones over again.

Gone with the Wind was one of the longest books I had ever laid eyes on that wasn't a history or a Bible. I knew the title from conversations about the movie. The cover made it look sexy, those flames and dark-haired lovers. My mother never had the time to censor what I could read, so at nine years old, I dove into Margaret Mitchell's epic of the Civil War.

Except it isn't. Written in 1936, *Gone with the Wind* predates the concept of Young Adult literature, or really even the idea of a young adult. But as the novel begins, Scarlett O'Hara is a sixteen-year-old girl caught between two cultures and about to embark on the greatest adventure of her life. If that's not YA, I don't know what is. It indulges in some of the most common trope constructions of the genre: Scarlett isn't beautiful, except that she definitely is. She is torn between two love interests who are both very attractive but appeal to different parts of her nature. She is set against insurmountable odds yet gifted with privileges of which she is never made aware. She proves astonishingly competent at skills never taught to her: mathematics, running a business, shooting a trained soldier in the face. Scarlett O'Hara is Katniss Everdeen in a hoop skirt. I fell in love with this book.

Scarlett was easy to identify with: bratty, cunning, manipulative, emotionally turbulent, artificially disguised as a victim. She flouts social convention and disagrees with the limits set for her by a restrictive society and a boring family. As a burgeoning preteen, this was like catnip. The short sex scenes were smoldering promises of what was to come in my own sex life. I read these scenes in that deliciously furtive way that kids do, trying to discern the mechanics from flowery euphemisms. I wept over the personal and political tragedies of Scarlett's life like they were my own. I was hooked.

I read *Gone with the Wind* the first few times as all kids read books: innocently. I did not yet know how to evaluate assertions or assumptions in fiction, to discern through an author's use of tone what she valued and what she despised. I did not yet have the tools to understand the book's racist content or consider my dissimilarities to Scarlett O'Hara. I was her and she was me and that was it. I entered adolescence with this book as my sorting hat. In the same way people use the Harry Potter houses to decide who among their friends is a Slytherin or a Gryffindor, I divided the girls I knew into Scarletts or Melanies, boys as either Ashleys or Rhetts. The Hufflepuff types around me were minor characters: the India Wilkses and Charles Hamiltons.

I came back to *Gone with the Wind* as a teenager, finally in early womanhood as Scarlett is in the first section of the novel. This reread was brought on by scarcity; I was losing my home. It was not the first time. I can't count the number of times we were evicted, either formally by a landlord or informally by family or my mother's partners, but I was familiar with the process at this point. I crammed all I could into my backpack and prepared to leave a place and never return. On this occasion, I was the last one in the house. My mother's boyfriend, who owned the place, had gone for the weekend, having made it clear that he wanted to return to his home with all traces of my mother and her children gone from it. When my work of packing up was done, my mother was supposed to come pick me up.

She didn't.

The electricity had been turned off and the cupboard was bare. I was no stranger to these conditions, either. I lay down on a couch in a back room without supper, lit a candle, and began to read. The book on the top of my pack was *Gone with the Wind*.

This time, I expected to identify with Scarlett in the postwar years at Tara. After all, she was starving. She had to pick cotton to survive. She was saddled with her mentally ill father and functionally orphaned by her mother's death. She had nothing, yet her indomitable spirit carried her through and back to prosperity.

At least, that was what I remembered.

Instead, for the first time, I began to dislike Scarlett. I saw how privileged she was. She owned a home and a farm that could not be taken from her, even by the tax collector. She had literal slaves to contribute labor to her household, who were inexplicably devoted to her as if she were their own child rather than the issue of two rich white people. She had family who loved her, including the unfailing sweetness of her despised sister-in-law, Melanie Wilkes.

The first time I read "I'll never go hungry again," I cried. I was a baby feminist and I saw only a stubborn, brave woman following her ambition and refusing to suffer the slings and arrows of outrageous fortune.

This time, I laughed. Yes, Scarlett is stubborn. Yes, she basically decides to resort to sex work in order to keep her property. But she has no idea that she's still a princess in this ruined kingdom. When Scarlett adds up her assets after this declaration, she has the cold eye of a jeweler considering a flawed gem: she has her own prettiness, a pair of diamond earrings, and a set of velvet drapes hanging in her house. Her million-dollar estate, populated and run by three unpaid human slaves, are not included in her inventory, even as she plans to gather up most of them and travel to Atlanta to engage in the aforementioned sex work. She is so blinded by her privilege that even in her ruinous state she cannot see these things for what they are: the unearned gifts of her station.

By the light of a candle, I laughed in a house with no heat as the snow fell outside. My laugh echoed in the empty darkness where no family or friend might have heard me. Certainly no domestic servants came to ask what was wrong and whether I maybe needed some corn whiskey or warm milk to calm me down.

I was not Scarlett O'Hara. I never would be. She was just another rich bitch who had no idea how lucky she was.

I read the novel again in college, my own postwar period. I had dropped out of high school and failed to launch. I had passed through several periods of homelessness, reading *Gone with the Wind* in starlight as it filtered through an olive grove, hoping not to be hassled by the cops. When I was hungry, I would read the passage about Scarlett's hunger at postbellum Tara, where she dreams of feasts of the past. I can recite that section from memory:

> How careless they had been of food then, what prodigal waste! Rolls, corn muffins, biscuit and waffles, dripping butter, all at one meal. Ham at one end of the table and fried chicken at the other, collards swimming richly in pot liquor iridescent with grease, snap beans in mountains on brightly flowered porcelain, fried squash, stewed okra, carrots in cream sauce thick enough to cut. And three desserts, so everyone might have his choice, chocolate layer cake, vanilla blanc mange and pound cake topped with sweet whipped cream. The memory of those savory meals had the power to bring tears to her eyes as death and war had failed to do, had the power to turn her ever-gnawing stomach from rumbling emptiness to nausea.

I would consider my own prodigal wastes: the last few cold fries I had thrown away when they failed to entice me, or the burnt edge of a frozen pizza cut off and tossed in the trash. I would read this section again and again, thinking of Thanksgiving dinners given by parents of friends who'd invite me out of pity. The fast food jobs I had had that included a discounted meal during my shift. Once I knew Scarlett for a spoiled brat, there was no going back. But at least I could suffer hunger with the O'Haras instead of suffering it alone.

It did not occur to me to ask how hungry her slaves were. When the household suffered food shortage, how did it affect those who had always received the scraps of the table? I was hungry like Scarlett was hungry: in a way that did not consider other people.

Community college taught me to read critically, and then to read as a writer. I began to pick apart the choices Mitchell made. As my racial consciousness was shakily born, I began to encounter *Gone with the Wind* as a cultural touchstone of whiteness. I saw the reverent references to it in other works: in *Prince of Tides*, in *Divine Secrets of the Ya-Ya Sisterhood*. Southern writers of the next generation held Mitchell blameless and enshrined her as the keeper of the Old South's identity. In doing so, they helped preserve the myth of the happy slave, the people who had made the whole story happen without ever existing at its center.

Additional works in the same universe failed in the same way to examine the book's relationship to whiteness. Critical disasters in every sense of the word, *Scarlett* and *Rhett Butler's People* were pale and puny fanfic-quality imitations of Mitchell's competent prose that also took no action to advance the storylines of any of the black characters beyond their subservient roles in the original. Only Alice Randall's unauthorized parody, *The Wind Done Gone*, does any of that work, and the Mitchell estate did everything in its power to try to stop that racial recontextualization and queering of the original novel from happening.

It was in reading these other books that I began to see the irony in my love and rejection of Scarlett O'Hara. I wasn't her; I wasn't born to privilege, a slave owner, a rich widow who was neatly handed the tools for triumph during the only adversity she had ever experienced. As a poor white woman, I was more like the O'Hara's unfortunate neighbor, Emmy Slattery, who attempted to buy Tara when Scarlett was down on her luck. As a fat woman working in food service and manual labor, I was more like Mammy: seizing my dignity by force of will beneath the yoke of terrible oppression. As a self-made success, I was more like Rhett Butler, who made his living as a gambler and discarded the morality of his culture to live as a hedonist and drunkard.

Except I was none of those characters. I was, in fact, Scarlett O'Hara.

The last time I read this book, I was older than Scarlett will ever be. The novel ends when she is twenty-eight, estranged from her husband, and the negligent mother of three children, one of whom has died. She has not grown up or learned anything from her mistakes. She is still a spoiled brat, insisting that she will get what she wants in the final words of the book. Because she has never known a life where that isn't the case.

Rereading is a way of encountering your former selves, tucked neatly between the pages like pressed spring flowers and autumn leaves. If you are honest and your memory is good, your former selves will speak to you as if this often-thumbed volume is your own diary. The last time you passed through this story, you were someone else. Because I have now read it over a hundred times in thirty years, *Gone with the Wind* holds many, many versions of me.

It holds my youngest conscious self, the one who had just begun to experience lust and doubt and accept that I am separate from the universe and subject to it. It holds my teenage self, trapped in homelessness and loneliness and searching for a way out, even if it means following Scarlett's blueprint of marrying young for a shot at a soft bed and some hot meals. It holds the dawn of my adult consciousness, when I was finally able to see the way this story is tilted to keep Scarlett always in focus and deprive slave characters of any equivalent humanity in the narrative.

Finally, in this last read, I was able to grapple fully with my own privilege and lifelong investment in white supremacy. I am ashamed to say that I never understood how truly hollow and mean-spirited the archetype of the Southern Belle is until I saw a comic of the ubiquitous hoop skirt made up of a slave ship in the article "The Southern Belle is a Racist Fiction" in 2014. I had thought (as most white liberals often think) that I was good enough, antiracist enough, that I was not invested in racist fictions anymore, and that I did not derive benefits from slavery and the structural forms of inequality that followed it in in my everyday life. These, too, are racist fictions. It took me far too long to see that even my optimism was a gift that helped me move toward the life I wanted.

American schoolchildren are taught a sanitized version of their own history, one that corresponds neatly to *Gone with the Wind*. We are induced to believe that many slaves were happy, treated as members of the family, and were transported out of Africa as "workers." We are told that everyone has been equal since 1776 and free since 1865, glossing briskly over the struggles of 1965 with a video of Martin Luther King delivering a speech that solved racism so that Obama could be elected in 2008. Congratulations, it's a postracial America! We are taught, explicitly and implicitly, that anyone who says different is just complaining because life is hard for everybody.

As the product of this myth treated as truth, of the policies of redlining and disenfranchisement and brutality that are the legacy of this American mythology, all white Americans are complicit. We are all Scarlett O'Hara. Some of us are Scarlett at her richest and most viciously powerful: Ivanka Trump in a ball gown thinking herself the favorite child of a self-made man who tells it like it is. Some of us are postwar Scarlett, taking an inventory of our privilege and remaining blind to over half of it being the product of plunder.

When I thought of myself as rising from the ashes of a ruined life and congratulating myself on digging my way out of poverty, going to college, rising to my own well-earned pride, I did not realize for many years that much of what came my way was luck. It was unearned privilege. Doors were open for me when they remained closed to others because I am white. Because I am not disabled. Because I am not trans. I worked hard just as Scarlett worked hard. But it took witnessing her ignorance for me to realize that I was also standing on someone's back to reach these heights. The trouble with most white Americans is that we never look down.

I have read *Gone with the Wind* over a hundred times. I have seen countless stories and videos that strive to explain who these angry poor white people are who elected Trump and insist on border walls and believe that abortion is murder and vote time and time again to keep themselves in poverty so long as their black neighbors suffer just a little worse than they do. I have spent my life in the presence of white feminists who have only read *Gone with the Wind* once and never got past the initial rush: what a trailblazer Margaret Mitchell was! Scarlett O'Hara is #goals! The O'Haras are the blueprint for the temporarily embarrassed millionaire: dirt-poor but still better than you because of how they were born. *Gone with the Wind* sells the white bootstrapper myth as romantic reality for white people. It has been doing it for nearly a century and it can be found in every bookstore, every thrift store, and every library in America.

It takes real work, as a white person, to realize the racism in which you have been steeped all your life. It takes rereading the texts you hold most dear. It takes literacy and critical thinking and listening to people of color to realize that not only is *Gone with the Wind* fiction, but most of what you know is fiction. Your family history is fiction. Your elementary school textbooks are fiction. Your construction of yourself is fiction. We all have to read ourselves more than once. We have to proofread and edit ourselves. We have to rewrite ourselves every day. We have to learn to separate truth from fiction from fake news. This is a monumental task, and most of us will fail.

Kids and adults will continue to pick up *Gone with the Wind* for the first time. It is in some little girl's hands right now, and she's seeing the world through Scarlett O'Hara's eyes.

I hope she goes back and reads it again.

Such People in It

GREEN AND RED SPECKS spun on the wall behind the karaoke stage. The effect was meant to be cheerful for the season, but it only made Omar think shitty Matrix Christmas as he slurped the last of his warm beer. He'd made the single glass last most of the night, knowing that he could only afford two and if he let his glass sit empty, the bartender would hustle him out.

Besides, his song hadn't come up yet.

Now the green and red geometry specks were swarming on a girl. She wore her long, red hair in two braids. That was a little racy, but it was a Friday night after all. The Decencies would have better things to do on a night like this, so the girl could probably squeak by. As long as she had her escort with her.

Synth-scat started up over the speakers, and Omar knew the song. Over the intro, the girl crowed into the mic, nearly swallowing its bulbous head.

"Sing along if your daddy tried to fuck you. Wave your hands in the ayy-err if he succeeded." She was drunk, but the entreaty landed well in the darker corners of the bar. Faceless patrons offered her some stamping and a number of low, wolfy whistles.

The girl was young and her voice was high. She forced it low, gravelly, trying to hit the opening line. "Janie's got a gun," she growled out. "Janie's got a gun."

No hands were waved in the air. The sole other woman in the bar sang along, staring down into her drink.

Omar signaled the bartender that he'd like that second beer now, please.

The next morning, Omar realized that he missed the feeling of being hungover. Not the headache like a rusty nail in the eyelid or the nausea that came and went like a siren sounding off in his gut. Just the selfish, bleary-eyed entitlement to be an asshole. The right to wear sunglasses indoors and see people give him a wide berth, perhaps a raised eyebrow over the coffee machine.

But that wouldn't do at all these days. Instead, he showed up to work in his pressed shirt and a tie from an acceptable American brand. His hair had been cut within the last two weeks, per city ordinance, and he had chosen Caucasian cut pattern #4. It worked best with his glasses. The mirror in his cubicle was mounted low, so that he could only see the bottom half of his own face.

"On the phone, people know if you're smiling," Ashton had said. "They can hear it." And so the mirrors had appeared one day, about the size of a chocolate bar, or the smartphone Omar used to have. In the sliver of mirror, Omar slapped on his grin. He cold-called leads for his company's software platform for the next fourteen hours. Most of the numbers on his lead gen list were disconnected. He ticked them off, one by one, and ate his peanut butter sandwich in slow, round bites between calls.

Ben strolled over sometime after sundown. "Do you want to come to supper tonight?"

Omar jumped in his chair, which gave a low squeak.

"Sorry, man." Ben smiled a little, fidgeting with the edge of his sweater vest. "But Katya thought it might be nice for you. You know. Home cooked meal and all that."

"Katya?" Omar looked up at his old friend. Ben's blue eyes were watery and he had lost weight.

"You know. Katy. She thought it was cool to go back to her roots." Ben stopped fidgeting. His arms seemed to hang on him like they were held on with pins.

"I didn't know she was Russian."

"Well, Ukrainian. It's all the same. So, you in? We've got a chicken." Ben's face brightened a little. A whole chicken for three adults and three kids was a big deal, good enough to be a holiday dinner.

"What's the occasion?" Omar tried to seem pleased at the invitation, though he knew he wouldn't go. Ben knew that, too.

"A little lottery money." Ben's grin faded. "So, what do you say?"

"Nah, but thanks, man. I'm gonna head home."

Ben patted the flat space where his belly used to be. "More chicken for me I guess." As he walked away, Omar could see that Ben had patched the holes in his shoes with rubber cement, probably from the supply room. Omar had no interest in reporting his friend for the paltry reward it could net him, but at the same time it seemed like something he might want to store for later.

He filed that away and swallowed the bile that rose in his throat just after.

He would have liked to have joined them for dinner. Just the thought of a chicken filled his mouth with juicy, acidic wanting. He liked Katy . . . or Katya, and hadn't seen her since the last game.

But they were gonna play again soon.

In the brief mirror, Omar unclenched his smiling jaw and pain flooded back into the right side of his mouth. He had looked with a flashlight and the mirror in his bathroom a hundred times. One molar back there was collapsing in on itself, like demolition in blackening slow motion. The pain was constant and sometimes bright enough to blind him. When he slept, he packed a cold shred of a wet rag in his mouth and positioned himself gingerly so that nothing would touch that side of his face and wake him in the night.

He hadn't told anyone and didn't want his friends seeing him struggle with the pain to eat a hot, moist, delicious mouthful of chicken. It would only worry and hurt them. There was nothing they could do.

Omar's hope was that the tooth would eventually rot out entirely or crack into pieces that he could remove with his pliers. He didn't look forward to that day, but that was the best possible outcome. It could also abscess and kill him with fever. From that angle, the pliers looked good.

His motorpool would not wait. He logged himself out with the others on second shift just as the third shift was moving in. The car was packed tonight, with seven thin adults crammed together in the wheezing old Prius. As the car struggled up the on-ramp, Omar saw candlelight through the plastic windows of an old city bus beneath the freeway. He wondered if a family lived there. The light disappeared as they climbed and accelerated into the night.

Omar woke up on Saturday earlier than he needed to. It was the damned tooth again. The pain was sharp, and he could not transmute it into any other sensation with the desperate alchemy he had been forcing for months now. Today had to be the day.

He checked the clock and saw that he had three hours yet before his alarm would have gone off. It would have to be enough. If he bled, he could pack his jaw. If people could hear his grimace over the phone, so be it.

When he had hidden the last half pint of whiskey in his freezer three years ago, he had tucked it in the far back, behind some lamb chops and bags of frozen peas. Things had been scary then, but not bleak. He was concerned but not terrified. He had teased Jennifer for her paranoia, back in those days.

He opened the freezer door and saw the flat bottle plainly, sitting beside an ice cube tray and a block of white corn that he had cut off the cob when it was cheap in the summer and pressed into a cube, trying to think ahead. He was saving it to eat over the holidays.

He drank three swallows of the whiskey right away, feeling the alcohol hit his empty stomach and light his veins as his body was still waking. Good.

The pliers were already in the medicine cabinet. There were two empty orange bottles there, both with Jennifer's faded name on them. He took care not to knock them over as he pulled his tool out.

Omar sat down on the closed lid of the toilet with a towel spread in his lap. He probed the collapsing tooth gingerly. Pain exploded through his jaw and he shut his eyes tight, sucking in air. He took another drink and a few deep breaths.

By feel, he was able to position the pliers' grippy jaws on either side of the offending molar. He pulled his glasses off when he realized that tears were pooling between the glass and his face, dropping them in the sink. Normally, Omar treated his glasses with something approaching reverence, but agony made him careless. Slowly, with a shaking hand, he brought the pliers together.

Every sound, every impact, every minute movement seemed to channel itself into the nerve at the root of that rotten tooth. He was whimpering like a dog. He thought *Inshallah* for half a second before yanking with his good right hand. His tongue lifted a tiny fraction as if to utter the last syllable of the illicit word.

When Omar came to, he was angled off the toilet seat with his face pressed to the wall in front of him. Blood dripped down the chipped and faded satin paint job and he had spotted his shirt. He knew immediately the tooth had not come cleanly out, because when he inhaled, he felt it shift excruciatingly in its loosened socket. He sat back, panting, nearing shock. He poured the rest of the whiskey into the other side of his mouth, letting it course down his throat mixed with his own blood. He swallowed, then reached in with his fingers and twisted the tooth free.

Blood poured out onto his hand where the cracked and blackened piece of bone lay. He had time to wonder how something so small could hurt him so badly, but the world turned brown and he sank sideways to the floor.

Omar awoke again with his neck cranked to one side against the tub and his face stuck to the floor in drying blood. He tore his clothes off and climbed into the shower, unconcerned that the hours for hot water had already passed.

He knew he was late. He knew he had missed his motor-pool. He dressed hastily and packed a clean sock in his mouth. He locked his door, leaving the gruesome mess for later, and headed to the main road to walk to work.

It was noon before he arrived. Omar clocked in, accepting that he would be docked seven hours' pay for showing up five hours late. It was worth it, since calling in sick on a Saturday would almost surely get him fired.

Ben came by with his face set in lines of worry sometime around three. He hung on Omar's cubicle wall, trying to avoid being heard.

"Where the hell were you?"

Omar squished one side of his face wetly, pointing to the wad of sock in his mouth. "I had a shmall prollem," he slurred.

"Oh shit," Ben said, his eyes widening. "Are you OK?"

Omar nodded. "I got it out. I'm gonna be OK."

"I have ibuprofen at my desk," Ben said hurriedly. "I got it when I broke my arm, but it's probably still good. I've been saving it. I'm gonna bring you some."

"Bleshoo," Omar said. He made two calls after Ben walked away. Both numbers were disconnected.

His friend came back a moment later with five precious little mauve pills tucked into his pasty hand. He laid them on Omar's desk. "Definitely take one now," he said. "But try to make them last."

Omar reached out to his friend with his dry hand, his phone hand. "Thank you."

Ben nodded. "Come home with me tonight," he said. "I insist. The game is tomorrow, and Katya is making potato soup. I bet you could eat that."

Omar's stomach growled audibly, as if it understood the conversation. He had not eaten since yesterday's peanut butter sandwich, not counting his breakfast of blood and whiskey. He nodded.

Saturday nights at the office were a combination of festal and exhausted. Everyone was excited to have their Sabbath day off. This week was even better, since Monday was Christmas.

"Everyone enjoy your two-day weekend," Ashton crowed as he waved people out the door. "And have a very blessed Christmas as we celebrate the birth of our savior!"

Omar ducked his head. Ben covered for him. "Blessed Christmas to you, Mr. Cumberland. Thank you for this excellent week."

Ben pressed himself into the back seat of the motorpool, letting Omar have the window. Omar pushed his face against the cold glass and thought he must be getting better. Or the ibuprofen was working. He planned to take another when he lay down that night.

Katya had indeed made potato soup. She sat Omar down on the couch and fussed over him, covering him with a blanket, setting him up with a tray, blending his bowl of soup so he wouldn't have to chew even the softest of bites of potato.

They all sat on the couch. Katya and Ben shared a blanket. Their three children were already tucked in bed and Omar was glad not to see them.

Katya looked as beautiful as ever. She wore her blonde hair up and out of her face in the frank privilege of her own home. She used the same mandated cosmetics as any woman Omar had seen in recent months, but she seemed more skilled with it. A few times, Omar had glimpsed faces through the windows of women's motorpools, their mouths like sore pink slashes, their eyes buttered in black. Almost as if they used their requirements with menace rather than compliance.

But Katya was all softness and welcoming. He thought she might be pregnant again, but it was early yet if it was true. Even her voice was milder than he remembered it.

"I can't believe you did that with pliers," she said. "How very brave."

Omar smiled weakly. "The soup's good, Katy. Thank you." He couldn't let the hot food touch the ragged hole where his tooth had been. But the ragged hole where his stomach lived was determined to find an alternate route.

"Katya," Ben reminded him, putting a hand on his wife's knee.

"I'm sorry. Katya."

"No need to be sorry," she said, pushing on errant hair out of her face and back into place. Omar thought the gesture looked strangely prideful. "I've just been learning more and more about my Russian heritage. I got the kids into a playgroup where they speak English and Russian, to give the kids a leg up when they get into high school and college. You know how it is."

Omar nodded. He did know.

"Too bad Marcus and his wife left the neighborhood," Ben said. "You know she used to be a dental assistant? We could have used her help with this."

Omar said nothing. Katya looked away. Marcus and his wife had "left the neighborhood" on the same day as Jennifer. Maybe Ben had forgotten that.

"Well, I'm sure you'll recover just fine," Katya said. "Remember when people used to take all those crazy shots and pills that didn't do anything at all? Or they made your kids retarded? At least now we all have a choice."

"We sure do," Omar slurred. He tipped up his bowl, finishing his soup. It was as good as it could have been, without fresh milk to make it creamy. Katya had clearly been saving bones to make broth.

There was no offer of seconds. There was no bread, and no dessert.

Eight o'clock rolled around and their daily broadcast tripped the TV and turned it on. They all stood for the national anthem, got the latest news of the war and the stock market, and a brief message from the president. The man looked saggier than usual; clearly the office was taking its toll after eleven years. Still, the old bluster and swagger was there. He promised them greatness and prosperity, reminded them of how bad things had been without law and order, and warned them not to become his enemies. It was the same speech as always, except for his parting words.

"I want to wish you all the best, the merriest Christmas. It's really an incredible thing to say that we're finally united as a nation behind one god, one holiday, and that we don't have all this stuff dividing us anymore. Not as a nation, and not as a world. We have peace on earth and good will toward men. Peace like my weak predecessors never could have achieved. We have incredible peace, peace like no other. And you know why we have that? Because America is great again. Just like I promised. God bless America, and goodnight."

"That almost sounded unscripted there, at the end," Ben mused. "Like he used to do."

Omar has stared at the floor during the broadcast. He didn't speak or look at the screen as long as the system was activated. People said it only listened when it was turned on, and Omar hoped that was true.

Katya gave him more blankets and he stretched out on the couch. He slept pretty well, all things considered.

In the morning, Ben was up early and already excited. "I've got the terra cotta heaters set up in the basement," he told Omar breathlessly. "Aaron and David are already on their way over, and they're bringing their wives to hang out with Katya, and their kids to play with Bonnie and Rhett and Gerald. We're all set."

Omar smiled weakly. His jaw was still sore, but the urgent, piercing pain was gone. He would actually get better. He was fairly sure of it.

He stood up and folded the blankets Katya had given him. He washed his face and pulled the sock out of his mouth to wash it. He rinsed his mouth with cold water, and then with salt water to ward off infection. The hole seemed huge and too red, too deep. But it wasn't really bleeding anymore. Small favors, he guessed.

Aaron and Deborah arrived first, their seven kids all piling out of the motorpool like a dishwasher pumping out foam. They ran for the house and Katya caught the littlest ones in her open arms. Deborah was definitely pregnant again, her face swollen to twice its normal size. She eased herself down onto the couch, nodding to the other men present. They nodded back.

Omar had known Aaron and Deb since college. He remembered that they were both fierce huggers back then. He had been at their wedding and they at his. There once were photos of Deb kissing the side of Omar's face, drunkenly. Jennifer had pulled that framed photo off the wall, but she had done it too late. Aaron had reported it as a property crime already. Omar could hardly look at his old friend, who had started to go bald prematurely. Good.

David and Liz arrived almost an hour later, coming from far outside the city. David had scored a job as a factory foreman, but it meant that they had to live out in the sticks. They had four children but would have no more. Liz had had a hysterectomy a year ago, following cancer. Omar didn't know how David had paid for it, but they had come through. They were thin and brittle and gimlet-eyed, but they lived. They lived together.

David walked over and shook Omar's hand manfully. "Old friend," he said. "What have you done to your face?"

"You should see the other guy," Omar said, his mouth like a crime scene.

David grinned. "I'm glad you came. I wasn't sure . . ." He glanced over his shoulder. Liz raised a hand to Omar. Her kids ran to the back room where the sound of children was rising to a shriek.

Katya directed the men downstairs. She had laid them a fair feast of baked potato skins, fried corn, cabbage chips, and six precious beers on ice.

Omar squinted a little, remembering the piles of pizza boxes, the bags of chips, the oceans of beer these gatherings once boasted. Upstairs, among the murmur of women's voices, he pretended he could hear Jennifer's, too. He sank into his chair, on the same side of the table as always.

Ben set up his screen and tumbled out his dice. They picked up their character sheets from their last game six months ago. They reviewed where they were in the quest.

"I point to the path in the forest and suggest the party move east," Aaron said confidently.

"I pick up the rear to keep the party safe," David added.

"I consult the map to see if that makes sense," Omar said gently. "Weren't we headed toward a tower?"

"You can see the tower above the trees," Ben said eagerly.

"We walk toward it," Aaron announced for everyone.

They made their way through the thicket to the base of the white stone tower.

"The doorway is intricately carved with runes."

"I read the runes," Aaron said, eagerly.

"Not so fast," Ben told him. "Roll intelligence plus linguistics. Difficulty six."

Aaron rolled enough successes to read the script, cheering at the clatter of dice on the table.

Omar smiled. The magic was beginning to work. His jaw hardly hurt at all anymore.

Ben shuffled through his papers and pulled a sheet free.

> If entrance to the tower you seek
> Through the eyes of the troll you must peek
> And if he deems you worthy still
> Unlock the tower's door he will.

Ben beamed over his little bit of doggerel.

"Come on," David said. "A fucking troll?"

Ben laughed a high-pitched trolling laugh. "It is I! Baltarias the forest troll. Only one of you may enter, and it is he who answers my riddle." Ben rubbed his hands together as if expecting a pot of gold rather than an answer.

Upstairs, the clumping of children's feet sounded as though they had decided to run like a herd of deer toward the back yard.

"I am owned by the poor; the rich does not need me. If you eat me, you will die! What am I?"

Omar rolled his eyes. "Ah, Baltarias! You have chosen a very old riddle indeed. Even I, a warrior with no book learning at all, know the answer. It is nothing!"

"Fie!" Ben cried, stretching the word out in his troll voice. "Fie! Fie a thousand times!" He cleared his throat and returned to his own voice.

"The door swings open."

"I check that it's safe before heading up the stairs," Omar says.

"We'll wait here for you." David consulted his character sheet again.

"Great."

"The staircase is dark and winding," Ben said.

"I keep my hand on the wall to be sure of my footing," Omar said, his excitement growing.

"You hear a strange sound coming from the top of the tower. You enter the room and see a beautiful princess, sitting in a chair and crying."

Omar blinked a moment. "I approach her carefully. I tell her, 'I am Antinous, the warrior. I have come to rescue you.'"

Ben softened his mouth, preparing to take on the role of princess. "She has big brown eyes and beautiful chocolate-brown skin," he began. "She looks up at you and says—"

"There can't be a black princess," Aaron complained. "Come on. Make her look like Galadriel."

Ben's eyes darted to his friend. "Come on Aaron, it's—"

"It's just not realistic," David said, kindly. "We're on a quest in a magical land that's closest to medieval Europe."

Omar looked at Ben, pursing his lips. "It's OK, Ben. I'm not here for real life."

Aaron looked away. David studied his character sheet closely.

Ben sighed, sinking down behind his screen. "The princess has luminous blonde hair, and otherworldly blue eyes," he began again.

The magic did not return. Omar accepted the princess's enchanted ring and let Aaron lead the party until sundown. Katya made a huge dinner of pasta for the army assembled. The kids sat on the floor. The adults gathered around the table and pretended they did not miss wine. They shied away from the harder subjects. The women spoke as little as possible and started clearing immediately once they had finished eating.

They all stood for the evening broadcast. It was brief, given the holiday. Omar looked at the floor, but his friends' hands clasped with those of their wives and children in his eyeline made him ache. He looked at the ceiling instead.

He said his goodbyes as they wiped the children's faces and gathered their things. The wives said goodnight at chaste distances from one another's husbands and Omar did not cast his mind back. He jammed his tongue into the hole where his tooth had been. They arranged their motorpools and disappeared into the night.

Omar went home alone. He had forgotten about the slaughterhouse conditions of his bathroom until he stepped in there to take a piss. He sighed at it, pissed anyway, and promised himself he'd spend Christmas Day cleaning it up.

He set up his computer and waited for the hum to tell him he had internet access. He dialed in and waited. At the stroke of midnight, his connection was approved. There was shuffling and roll-calling on the other end for a moment before the tired, smiling face of his wife appeared.

"Hi, honey," he told her, his whole heart shooting up into his face like a popped cork.

"Hey, baby." Her full lips looked ashen. Her cheeks were hollow.

"How you doing out there?" The northeastern women's penal colony was somewhere in Vermont, but civilians were not permitted to know where. He could see her breath in little white puffs. It must be cold there, even inside.

"I'm surviving." She smiled a little for him. "Tell me about the girls."

Omar's jaw tightened before he could stop it and he winced in pain.

"Did somebody hit you?" Jennifer's brows came together and down. To the right or the left of her, some other woman was crying already.

"No, honey. Bad tooth, that's all." He cleared his throat. "I, uh. I haven't heard from my sister since October. The word was good then, but since . . . Since then I don't have anything."

Jennifer looked down into her lap. He could see her forehead wrinkling as she struggled with this disappointment. When she looked back up at him, it was as if the sun had risen. She had her hard look on, the one that made him think they could get through anything.

"That's what I get for having black girl babies whose last name means 'prosperous' in Arabic." She swallowed thickly, trying to strengthen her voice and smile again. "That's what I get for being a loud-ass instigator."

The shock came so quickly that she hardly finished the sentence. Omar didn't know if it had come because she had said 'ass' or 'Arabic.' The muscles in her neck jumped, and she shut her eyes tight.

"Careful now," he told her.

"Tell me something nice," she said.

"I saw some of our old friends yesterday," he said. The Andersons. And the Flemings. Over at the Weisses' house. Katy is 'Katya' now."

Jennifer rolled her eyes. "Remember the shit she gave Andrea, back in the day?" The shock was slower this time but seemed to last longer. Through the grainy resolution, Omar saw the shine of unshed tears in her eyes.

"Andrew," he said softly. "Andrew is in the camp in Oklahoma now."

Jennifer nodded, knuckling one eye. "One more nice thing. Before I have to go. Come on, baby."

"I love you," he told her, unable to come up with something lighter or more hopeful. "I love you so much. I wish you were here to put up all your old Christmas shit so I could complain about it."

That time the shock was so sharp he could hear her make a little sound in her throat.

"Wait, that was me! How can they—"

The transmission cut out. Jennifer's pained face disappeared. The power in the apartment cut out a moment later. Omar sat in the silence, his ears ringing, the hole in him throbbing without answer.

The bars opened again on the day after Christmas. Omar climbed the karaoke stage, when he was ready. It wasn't his song. He was supposed to be at work. He didn't care.

"Sing along if you're passing for white," he said over the calypso intro to "Kokomo" by the Beach Boys. "Throw your hands in the ayy-err if your reason for living is in an internment camp."

Heads that had been drooping popped up to look at him. The Decencies were already on their way, he was sure of it.

"If you had to smuggle your kids out of the country to keep them safe, lemme hear you say *yeah*!" Omar ignored the song entirely, just using the mic for the few moments that he could.

Nobody said "*yeah*." They stared at him as the electronic background singers warbled their way through the harmonies. They were watching him, all around the room. They were listening. There was a moment, just a fraction of a second, when it seemed that he could lead them, marching out into the street and toward . . . what? To Lansing, to raze the capital? Where could they go? What could they hope to achieve?

Omar thought of the families living under the freeway. He thought of his two daughters, somewhere in Lebanon, hopefully safe even though they'd never see their parents again. His sister had promised: his daughters were her daughters. He had at least achieved that.

The Decencies came through the door and moved toward the stage. He cupped the mic in both hands.

"Throw up a finger if you can still remember what it was like to be free!" He was roaring into the mic when the billy club hit him. He could have saved himself the trouble in pulling his tooth, after all.

Before he passed out, Omar could see through his one unswollen eye that four men in the bar had raised a finger, some of them hovering just above the rim of their glasses. Careful, but showing. Rising. Omar thrashed and fought as much as he could to keep the Decencies from seeing them, too.

"Sprawling into the Unknown"
Meg Elison interviewed by Terry Bisson

It's EELison, right?
It is. Every time I get asked if I'm Harlan's daughter, I wonder if there would have been any advantage in it.

Where are you from? Where are you headed?
I'm from everywhere; I grew up an army brat and got evicted a lot, and nowhere feels like home. The good thing about growing up like that is that I've always been able to say I'm headed somewhere better, and it's always been true. I'd like to think that I'm headed home, but I'll have to let you know when I've seen it.

Philip K. Dick Award! I'd say you hit the ground running. Was The Book of the Unnamed Midwife *your first try at a novel?*
I definitely did not expect to win an award with my debut novel. I hit the ground stunned, but running. This was, however, not my first novel. I wrote a truly execrable short novel when I was twenty-two that's like a shit salad with mortification for dressing. It will never see the light of day.

The unnamed midwife is pretty good with a gun. Are you?

I learned to shoot rifles when I was quite young. Picked up hand-guns as an adult. I'm not sure we should be allowed to own them, but for as long as we can I want to be good at it. So I practice with a secret lesbian gun collective and stay sharp.

Did the PKD change things for you?
It's hard to say. I know things would have been different if I hadn't won. Most indie books get very little press and make hardly any sales. I did it backward; I didn't have any short stories out before I published a novel. I didn't know the genre at all. I didn't know I was eligible for the Campbell/Astounding award until my eligibility had passed. I learned everything on the fly with an award-winning book on the market, without an agent or a Clarion class or a clue. But I snatched a brass ring with my very first piece of published fiction. I know that the award opened doors for me, that it made the career I have now possible. I don't know where I'd be now without it. It changed my life.

In San Francisco are you an immigrant or a native?
I wish I came from here. I meet people from here who are effort-lessly cool, with an innate sense of the topography and always knowing what neighborhood everything is in: upper and lower, inner and outer, right down to the block where the Tenderloin be-comes the Tenderknob. I think of San Francisco as a very beautiful woman who is completely out of my league. I follow her around, and I know everything about her that she'll let me know. But she'll never love me back. We'll never be intimate. I can't afford her, and she knows it. There's a poet named Nazelah Jamison who wrote

a poem about who Oakland is as a person, how accepting and chaotic and kind she is. Oakland isn't my city, either. But at least she's always glad to see me.

You are pretty prolific with short stories. Does that mean they are easy for you? Or just that there are lots of markets?
Short stories are easy for me. I get ideas for them all the time, typically knock them out in a single sitting, and I keep a couple of spreadsheets to track my submissions and publications. I love them as an art form: they can do one thing perfectly. I grew up reading short story authors like O. Henry and Shirley Jackson and Stephen King and yourself and Joan Didion, and I studied what they did, how they encapsulated a whole world in just a few pages. I wanted to do that, too.

But lots of markets? There are very few markets and they fold all the time. The word gets passed that *Playboy* and the *Atlantic* are buying fiction again, and I watch writers lick their chops thinking about paying the cell phone bill with a short story. They're challenging to write well, selling them is highly competitive, and at ten cents a word I'm barely beating Jo March in the nineteenth century. I must really love the form—there's no other compelling reason to go on.

Was getting published an ambition or a byproduct?
Getting published was the supreme ambition of my existence. I have terrible flight anxiety and it's gotten a lot better since I've been able to think to myself, *At least I've been published, so it's OK if I die*. It happened sooner and easier than I expected, and I ended

up sprawling into the unknown as if I was pushing against a stuck door and it suddenly flung open. Once you've achieved your life goal, what do you do then? Publish more, I guess. Set your cap for various lists and prizes and benchmarks. I wanted to see my name on covers, my book on library shelves, and reviews of my boiling brains in the papers. I got everything I wanted. I have been trying to aim higher ever since.

Do you think writers have a special responsibility? To whom or what?
There's this artist who works in mixed media, a Mexican named Jorge Méndez Blake. He created this piece of art that shows the impact of a book by jamming a copy of Kafka's *The Castle* into the first row of bricks in a wall. The book does not conform to brick shape, and the entire wall is warped around it. There's a ripple to its structure, and it's a powerful visual metaphor for the work that a book can do.

Throughout our history, books have done what kings and legislators and even the Bomb fail to do: they make people see things in a way they hadn't seen them before. That's an awesome power, and that must come with some responsibility. We are all responsible to the societies we inhabit; we make up the tenor and pace of life to the people around us. However, I don't think that a writer's responsibility is any greater than that of a pipefitter or a president. We are all bound to each other and are all capable of callous cruelty or kindness. Books are uniquely powerful—all art is. But writers are simply human. We are responsible for our work and ourselves. By the time our books are a brick in the wall, most of us are as dead as Kafka. And maybe half as well understood.

You are being deported from the USA. You are handed an envelope welcoming you to another country. What country are you hoping it's from?
The most practical choice for me is Germany. I speak the language, I am prepared to be a good part of a socialist society, and I've always felt quite welcome there. As much as I've always wanted to be a Brit, they've got a hell of a mess going over there right now. I loved my time in Mexico, and my Spanish is pretty good, but I could never get over the way men look right past me to speak only to my male companion. Germans are terribly polite. I could settle there quite well.

One sentence on each please: Rudy Rucker, Uber, Nell Zink.
I met Rudy at a party and I was struck by how vital and wry he is. He won the PKD the year I was born. I'm banned for life from Uber for writing about the CEO being less than honorable when I was a college journalist. Nell Zink's *Mislaid* is a hell of a book, and I'd like to make her a cocktail sometime.

Cliterary Salon. OK, I get it. But what's the deal?
Some friends of mine (Louis Evans, Lauren Parker, Maggie Tokuda-Hall) wanted to do a San Francisco LitQuake event that nobody else was doing, so we put together a feminist reading called ClitQuake. We packed the house two times in a row and decided to make it a monthly show, highlighting voices that don't always get to speak into a mic. We've been doing it for a couple of years now and it feels like pure glory. We make enough to pay the writers who perform. This city is rich with literary events, and I shine with pride that we get to be part of that.

*After two years at a college that nobody has ever heard of, you trans-
ferred to one that nobody has never heard of. What did Berkeley do
for you?*

That college that nobody has heard of had some of the best pro-
fessors I've ever studied with and set me up for success in ways
I can't ever pay back. They peened my logic and argumentation
until I could write clearly, concisely, and reason my way through
anything. I hope to someday make a large gesture of some be-
nevolent kind to Mt. San Jacinto College. They deserve a lot of
recognition.

After I was properly prepared to receive, Berkeley gave me
everything. A million doors opened up to me that I couldn't even
have seen from where I was standing. MSJC taught me to write,
but Berkeley taught me to read. I'd never had instruction in close
and engaged reading like I got at Cal, and I had my nose forced
back to the page like it hadn't been since I learned to sound words
out. Learning to write was important, but there's nothing you can
do with it until you've learned to take a story apart and see how it
works. I published my first book within a month of graduating. It
was jet fuel on the fire of my voice.

What's hardest about being big?

Fitting in a fucking airline seat. I feel great, and I climb pyramids
and dance all night. I get all the attention I can handle. All I
want in this world are things that fit my body. Clothes. Chairs.
Bathtubs.

Where did you meet your husband?

My husband and I both dated the same girl in high school! She was a dragon-clawed goth queen, and I couldn't stand that he had her attention. Other things I couldn't stand: his highlights, his attitude, his letterman's jacket, his Mormonism. Things have changed a little since then.

Did you ever want to be small?
If I had it my way, I'd be much, much bigger. My true form is fifty feet tall and made of gold, shrieking like Godzilla and eating entire oyster beds.

You have been nominated for the Tiptree Award but now will never, ever win it. What went wrong?
Without in any way condoning the killing of a disabled spouse, I was troubled by the name change on the Tiptree. Sure, the tide is turning, and people are beginning to realize that there are no heroes, just people. But I couldn't help but notice that it takes a lot of high-profile agitating and protesting and insisting that we remove the name of a dead man from an award. Tiptree's legacy was as fragile as the legacies of women and queer people always are. We have to be perfect. Campbell had to be a fascist to get blowback. Lovecraft had to be a monster. Asimov's reckoning is never going to come, and he was a serial public assaulter. Women and queer people are almost always footnotes in science fiction history. Tiptree was imperfect and did a terrible thing. But now even the footnote that name held has gotten smaller.

What can you tell me about Layla?

Find Layla is the most deeply personal thing I've ever written. I grew up very poor and with criminally bad parents. I don't talk about it much, but I decided to work some of it out in fiction. Layla is the culmination of a lot of my worst stories. Also she swears like a sailor and does small crimes like I did as a kid. I feel naked looking at that book.

Like Hemingway, you often use simplicity as an ornament. Do you share his background in journalism?

I became obsessed with Hemingway when I was at Berkeley. I had this incredible professor, the late Ron Loewinsohn, who taught us *The Sun Also Rises*, and I got time alone with him in office hours. I asked him if the woman in the book, Brett, was meant to be read as barren as a foil to Ernie's ever-castrated heroes. It's the 1920s, she's fucking a nineteen-year-old bullfighter, and pregnancy never comes up. Loewinsohn blinked at me and told me he'd never thought about it. It was a seed for my first book.

From there, he taught me how to pick apart Hemingway's simplicity. The way he lays short phrases over one another like a net. The way he lets an image carry the scene without getting between the reader and what he wants the reader to see. Emerson's transparent eyeball. I had been working as a journalist for a year at that point, and I knew that's where Hemingway had cut his teeth, too. But factualism as a style is more than that. It doesn't just tell you the who/what/when; it puts you in the middle of it. Like anything great, it looks easy until you try to do it.

If you could read one other language fluently, what would it be?

Whatever the hell the Voynich Manuscript is written in. That thing drives me crazy. For everything else, there's Google Translate.

Is humor a sauce in your fiction, or an entrée?
Humor is a sauce. I'm not funny enough to make it the entrée. For that matter, I'm not smart enough to make science fiction the entrée, or romantic enough to make love the entrée. The story is always the main dish; I bought a whole chicken. I'm gonna slather it with something I like the taste of and serve it up hot.

My Jeopardy *answer: Five. You provide the question, please.*
I read this to my husband and he reminded me that I was knocked out of the *Jeopardy* qualifying rounds because I declined to study state capitals like he suggested. He further suggested I write up a question about state capitals to go with this answer. Once again, I decline.

What do you read for fun? And don't ask me what I mean by "fun." I ask the questions.
McSweeney's online stuff always makes me laugh or makes me think clever thoughts. I read *F&SF* every month with great joy and ceremony, in the bath with my phone shut off. I love John Scalzi and always find his work fun. Seanan McGuire is fun until she rips my heart out and makes me eat it. I love reading old joke books on Project Gutenberg and trying to figure out how humor and language change over time. And Carmen Maria Machado has skill and whimsical control that makes me scream—it's pleasurable, it's maddening, it's deep and connected to popular culture

and transcends genre. I can't keep quiet when I read her. I huff and I wheeze and I cheer. And N.K. Jemisin once wrote a fight scene (in *The City Born Great*) that made me stop in the middle of the financial district in San Francisco at 8:30 a.m. and howl like a wolf in my office clothes.

Have you ever been attacked by self-driving cars?
Not attacked, but late one night in San Francisco I saw a fleet of them being tested. Silent, gliding like black sharks through the night.

What kind of car do you drive? I ask this of everyone.
I drive a 2015 Nissan Versa that's covered in vinyls and quotes from Neil Gaiman's Sandman graphic novels. It gets me some of the oddest questions around town.

We met at a Locus Christmas party. I missed it this year (2019). How was it? How's 2020 shaping up for you?
We actually met at SF in SF, and I was blown away to see you there. One of your stories ("They're Made of Meat") gave me an out-of-body experience when I was fifteen and set the course of my career. But I was just another adoring fan, and you were very gracious and had no reason to know who I was at the time.

I love the Locus Christmas party, particularly for the reason that I meet people like you there. This year's was no exception. I had a long talk with Isaac Fellman and flirted abominably with Ellen Klages, who is a genius, and I'm not fit to touch the hem of her garment. Almost nothing I dreamed would be true about becoming a real writer turned out to be true; most of it was out of movies like *Romancing the Stone* or *Misery*. But the parties are every bit as grand, as sophisticated, as electrifying as I ever wildly fantasized. I party with the gods.

This year, 2020, is shaping up to be great and terrible, as only an election year can be. But I've got two books coming out, and three more in the chamber. It's good to be alive.

What question do you wish I had asked?
I'm just relieved you didn't ask me one of the four questions I always get. Terry, you're a treasure to the genre, and it is a great honor in my life to have you ask me about my car.

Guts

THE FIRST TIME IT happened, it was my mother. What perfect betrayal, like burning down the house where I was born. She grew tired in secret of the long, curved line of her belly, pendant in sweatpants and spreading over her lap when she sat. She hated huffing and puffing up the stairs, and she worried she'd become diabetic. So she underwent a radical form of weight-loss surgery that eliminated over half of her gut—and taught me a powerful lesson in how intolerable it was to be like me.

Four kids and a minivan—nobody expected her to bother about her looks anymore. She didn't tell anyone she was going to do it; she only told me I'd have to look after my younger siblings on the eve of the surgery. She made up her mind and didn't want their judgments or their approval. The week before was an orgy of overeating that I recall as a conveyor belt of food. Carbonara thick as oil paint on piles of handmade noodles. Pot roast in flour-thickened gravy, potatoes enough to starve the Irish again, followed by bacon sandwiches that blurted mayonnaise from every side when she bit into them.

Even then, she barely cleared the insurance company's weight requirement. Her doctor told her to make that last week count. Her best friend joked that she must be going in to get her tits done. She laughed and went under the knife at 4'11" and 285 pounds, nearly as wide as she was tall.

My mother was the first woman I knew who moved out of her own body. She vacated it, bit by bit: her lawn of her hair turning colors and falling out, the front porch of belly and breasts disappearing overnight, the foundation of muscle repossessed and leaving her to scoot down the stairs on her disorientingly bony ass. She disappeared. Her hair grew back, but her face changed shape so sharply that friends who she hadn't seen in a year did not recognize her. She was like any other woman; she loved the attention her new body received and being able to buy clothes in any store she saw.

But what she really wanted was to not be like me anymore.

I went to support groups with her in the year after the surgery. I didn't go for the endless stories of these recovering fatties who had traded the feeling of being squeezed by the outside world for being strangled to thinness from within. I didn't go for the stories of divorce so utterly rote and predictable that I struggled not to laugh. Men often marry fat women for very specific reasons. Conditions change and those men split like bananas. I went along because everyone there had once looked like me—and some of them had very nice clothes. They'd trade with one another, a 16 for a 14, a 12 for an 8. They shrank before my eyes like icicles in spring. The tables marked 26/24/22 filled up and there was no one else to take those elastic dresses and 3X yoga pants. I showed up with a roll of garbage bags.

More than once I inherited someone's favorite outfit in its entirety, replete with the story of how it made her feel. I would wear that outfit later and remember that she wanted to stop being this so badly that she let someone cut out a large section of her intestines. She had an anchor-shaped scar across her entire abdomen. She vomited every day and shit herself at least once a week, but at least, thank god, it was all worth it because she wasn't fat anymore.

There were other people I knew who moved out of their bodies, and I could understand why: They knew they had to go. They were being evicted anyway—blown knees and exhausted pancreas pushing them toward desperate measures. Weight-loss surgery seemed a fair price if the alternative was death.

But in nearly every case, the alternative was *my life*.

I used to joke with people that I was my mother's *before* picture, in the ubiquitous and devastating tradition of photos taken to reveal dramatic weight loss, the punchline for every ad that sells weight loss to women. *Before* we had shared a silhouette, titanic ass and Olympian hips, a pear-shaped and pendulous swing we rode through the world. *After* I had trouble believing we were the same species, let alone iterations of the same bloodline. Long legs and short arms, freckles, and the same crooked pinky finger. But disparity of scale suggested two different climates, two long-separated branches on the tree of life.

Before, my mother had dealt with the way people refuse to take fat women seriously. She had endured the infantilization and desexualization, and she was ready to trade it in. Two days after the surgery, she ignored her doctor's orders and tried to chug a Coke. I watched her stand over the kitchen sink with brown foam pouring from her nose and mouth, knowing herself chastened not by a paternalistic and fatphobic doctor for once, but by the physical reality that her new stomach was the size of a Dixie cup. A month later, I watched her black out after eating a Starburst; the sugar dumped into her bloodstream so fast that it acted like heroin when it hit her vitals. She traded the agony of perception for daily physical torment. After years of trying and failing at diets that never worked for anyone, she chose the nuclear option. She weighed her options and chose this over living a life like mine.

For me, it's only the surgery that achieves the sharp sensation of abandonment, rejection, and betrayal. I've seen friends through every diet, every justification of denial, misery, and elimination. A friend or a cousin will one day lose the ability to converse about anything but carbs or sugar or whole foods or animal products. I'll stop listening and start nodding. I know they're trying to move out, move away. They cannot bear to be what we are anymore.

The fat people who become obsessed with counting calories and steps, the ones who try to vacate their bodies a little at a time . . . I don't worry about them. They'll never make it. Sooner or later they all come back.

The ones who follow in my mother's footsteps are the ones that really leave. They get something cut up and cut out, they install new hardware to stop them from eating the world. They pack it in and they don't return. I stay me.

I'll be polite to my fellow fatties when they fall prey to the pressure. I understand what they're going through. Thin people talking diets fill me up with liquid murder. I cannot abide their careful warding, hanging up knots of garlic and crossing themselves three times when they see me coming. I will not listen to their terrified superstition or their smug pseudoscience when they tell me again and again what they are willing to go through rather than become like me. When their talk rolls around to calories and their moral obligation to hate themselves, I typically spread out as wide as I can. I can expand like a jellyfish; it is a particular advantage of the very fat. I conform to the shape of my container like a water balloon. Displaying maximum width, I'll eat anything I can get my hands on while they talk. On one notable occasion I shut down a discussion on the evils of white rice by calmly eating a trick-or-treating-sized bag of mini Snickers while nodding my fat head to show I understood.

In outraged weariness of being seen as a cautionary whale, I seek out ways to weaponize my own image. I haunt thin people at the gym as the Ghost of Fatness Yet to Come. It started off as a demoralizing phenomenon; I began by refusing to shrink away from the pained glances and open hostility I receive for having the audacity to live in a fat body without making a constant apology for myself. My gym in San Francisco is a caricature of bodily obses-sion. Its ad campaigns are notorious, and lithe trainers cruise the floor like sharks sniffing for blood. There are no other fat people there. An orca among eels, I cast my shadow over their swimming and striving, and they look upon me in naked terror. I am the reason they get up at 5 a.m. and wear a monitor that counts their steps. I am the worst thing that can happen.

One after another, the fat people in my life have left me. Not through diet or exercise, not through the much-vaunted "lifestyle change." They get the surgery and they cross over to the other side. Many of them have been self-accepting, even fat-positive. They came through hell to love themselves and live in their bodies without apologizing. But they've gotten tired of haunting the gym. They get tired of people lecturing and begging. They get tired of men at the bar shouting, "Man the harpoons." They get tired of their seatmates on airplanes asking to be moved. They get tired of hearing they were too fat to fuck, or that this dress does not come in that size. They've done the impossible math: one set of humiliations they're willing to trade for another. They come to agree with our thin friends: this life is the absolute worst fucking thing that can happen to a person.

I made new friends with a fat girl. She is beautiful and smart and holds an enviable position in my community. I tried several times to engage her in the casual sorority of fat girls, to talk brands and clothes and share a little eye roll at the way things are. She rebuffed me in a kind but cold way, and I didn't know why. I thought spitefully that she might be one of them, in long recovery from the knife and not yet passing for thin. Months later, she published her own story of dysphoria in a lyrical cry that broke my heart. I adjusted. I took another step in the direction the conclusion toward which most of my life has been leading me: No matter how much they hurt, the actions of others are entirely for and about themselves. They aim those harpoons at their own hearts.

My mother did not opt for invasive surgery to leave me behind. She did it because was tired of the inescapable fight that is life in a fat body. I am not the victim here. I am only a casualty.

Yet another friend went in for the surgery, early this year. I tried to look at her life without judgment, without centering my own emotions, and figure out why she would choose this. We're old enough now that vanity itself does not seem like enough.

Maybe she's lonely and thinks this is the answer. Maybe she wants to travel without being a spectacle and an inconvenience. Maybe she just wants to live in another body before she dies. In the end it doesn't matter. She's doing the thing that everyone but me will understand. It's what they would do in her place.

The first day I knew she was home and recovering, I briefly considered having a dozen donuts delivered to her door.

But I didn't. Because there are worse things a person can be than fat.

Bibliography

Books

The Road to Nowhere trilogy:

The Book of the Unnamed Midwife (Seattle: 47North, 2014).
The Book of Etta (Seattle: 47North, 2017).
The Book of Flora (Seattle: 47North, 2019).

Find Layla (Seattle: Skyscape, 2020).

Short Fiction

"Next of Kin," Vice.com, 2016.
"Personal Trainer," *Compelling Science Fiction* no. 2, 2016.
"Big Girl," *Fantasy & Science Fiction* 133, no. 5–6, 2017.
"Hysteria," Vice.com, 2017.
"In Loving Memory," in *Strange California*, edited by Jaym Gates and
    J. Daniel Batt (Charlotte, NC: Falstaff Books, 2017).
"The Middle Child," *Red Room* no. 1, 2017.
"Matchmaker," in *Hardened Hearts*, edited by Eddie Generous (British
    Columbia: Unnerving, 2017).
"Rapture," *Shimmer* no. 44, 2018.
"Endor House," *Lightspeed* no. 104, 2019.

"The Game Show," in *Wastelands: The New Apocalypse*, edited by John
    Joseph Adams (London: Titan Books, 2019).

"Hey Alexa," in *Do Not Go Quietly*, edited by Jason Sizemore and
    Lesley Conner (Toronto: Apex Publications, 2019).

"Portal," Vice.com, 2019.

"Safe Surrender," Slate.com, 2019.

"Familiar Face," *Nightmare* no. 90, 2020.

Essays

"On Decades of Diaries: Intimate, Profane, Honest," Literary Hub,
    LitHub.com, 2016.

"How Lwaxana Troi Became Our Space Aunt," StarTrek.com, 2019.

"How to Write a Book in Ten Days," Literary Hub, LitHub.com 2019.

"The Unicorn-like Creations of Moebius, Concept Artist," and "David
    Bowie's Queer Glam Futuristic Fashion," in *Lost Transmissions:*
    The Secret History of Science Fiction and Fantasy, edited by
    Desirina Boskovich (New York: Abrams, 2019).

"Writing with My Keys between My Fingers," *Uncanny Magazine* no.
    32, 2020.

About the Author

MEG ELISON IS A San Francisco Bay Area author. Her debut novel, *The Book of the Unnamed Midwife* won the 2014 Philip K. Dick Award and was a Tiptree longlist mention that same year. It was reissued in 2016 and was on the Best of the Year lists from Amazon, *Publishers Weekly*, *Kirkus*, and PBS. Her second novel was also a finalist for the Philip K. Dick Award. She has published short fiction and essays with *Slate*, *Lightspeed*, *Catapult*, *Electric Literature*, *Fantasy & Science Fiction*, *Shimmer*, and *McSweeney's*. Elison was the spring 2019 Clayton B. Ofstad endowed distinguished writer-in-residence at Truman State University, and is a coproducer of the monthly reading series Cliterary Salon.

PM Press is an independent, radical publisher of books and media to educate, entertain, and inspire. Founded in 2007 by a small group of people with decades of publishing, media, and organizing experience, PM Press amplifies the voices of radical authors, artists, and activists. Our aim is to deliver bold political ideas and vital stories to all walks of life and arm the dreamers to demand the impossible. We have sold millions of copies of our books, most often one at a time, face to face. We're old enough to know what we're doing and young enough to know what's at stake. Join us to create a better world.

PM Press
PO Box 23912
Oakland, CA 94623
510-658-3906 • info@pmpress.org

PM Press in Europe
europe@pmpress.org
www.pmpress.org.uk

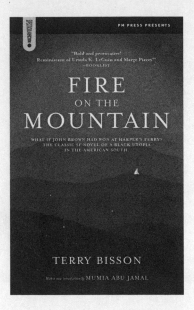

"Bold and provocative!
Reminiscent of Ursula K. LeGuin and Marge Piercy!"
—BOOKLIST

FIRE
ON THE
MOUNTAIN

WHAT IF JOHN BROWN HAD WON AT HARPER'S FERRY?
THE CLASSIC SF NOVEL OF A BLACK UTOPIA
IN THE AMERICAN SOUTH.

TERRY BISSON

With a new introduction by MUMIA ABU JAMAL

Fire on the Mountain

**Terry Bisson with an Introduction
by Mumia Abu-Jamal**
$15.95
ISBN: 978-1-60486-087-0
5 by 8 • 208 pages

It's 1959 in socialist Virginia. The Deep
South is an independent Black nation
called Nova Africa. The second Mars
expedition is about to touch down on
the red planet. And a pregnant scientist
is climbing the Blue Ridge in search of
her great-great grandfather, a teenage
slave who fought with John Brown
and Harriet Tubman's guerrilla army.

Long unavailable in the U.S., published in France as *Nova Africa*, *Fire on the
Mountain* is the story of what might have happened if John Brown's raid on
Harper's Ferry had succeeded—and the Civil War had been started not by
the slave owners but the abolitionists.

*"History revisioned, turned inside out ... Bisson's
wild and wonderful imagination has taken some
strange turns to arrive at such a destination."*
—*Madison Smartt Bell, Anisfield-Wolf Award
winner and author of* Devil's Dream